Emeralds in the Snow

by

Maggie Bishop

High Country Publishers, Ltd
Boone, North Carolina
2004

Published in the United States by:

High Country Publishers, Ltd
197 New Market Center #135
Boone, NC 28607
(828) 964-0590
Fax: (828) 262-1973

Library of Congress Cataloging-in-Publication Data

Bishop, Maggie, 1949-
  Emeralds in the snow / by Maggie Bishop
        p. cm.
  ISBN 1-932158-56-1 (trade pbk.)
  1. Sugar Mountain (N.C.)—Fiction. 2. Women teachers—
Fiction. 3. Treasure trove—Fiction 4. Ski resorts—Fiction. I.
Title.
  PS3602.I76E47 2004
  813'.6—dc22

2004010132

10 9 8 7 6 5 4 3 2

First Printing November 2004

Cover design: Aaron Burleson
Text design: schuyler kaufman

Acknowledgments:

Thanks to the following real people, whose names I used in this novel:

My parents, Pearle & Lyle Bishop;
Gunther Jochl, Sugar Mountain boss;
Dean Lyons, head of Ski Patrol at Sugar;
Jane & Bob Boyer, Sugar Ski Patrollers;
Joe White, Sugar groomer extaordinaire.

Thanks to these real people who helped with background, technical info, and photos:

Anne Whitton Boyvea, model for Emerald;
Dirk J. Krause, model for Lucky;
Judy Geary, editor;
George Ostrouchov, for providing math info;
Sgt. Frank Guy, Boone Police Department, handling the body
Authors B J Foster, schuyler kaufman, & Jane Wilson
Verda Ingle, for enrichment
Minnie Belle Francis, of Blowing Rock,
for permission to photograph Crystal Wedding Chapel;
Conard Rhymer for permission to photograph his house
JBH Imports in Boone, NC and Mike Vassil and Neta Bliss
of Grandfather Gem Mine & Shop, Foscoe, NC,
for permission to photograph their emeralds

Thanks to these organizations for training and support:

High Country Writers
Romance Writers of America
National Ski Patrol
Sugar Mountain Volunteer Ski Patrol

And to
Barbara & Bob Ingalls, publishers

Dedication:

To my husband
Bob Gillman,

*With my gratitude
for all your
Love and Support*

Emeralds in the Snow

by

Maggie Bishop

Prologue

Everett Graham cursed under his breath as his freshly-detailed blue Cadillac bounced sharply along the rutted road, kicking up a billowing cloud of dust behind it. This trip grew more irritating every time he made it. He longed to send an asphalt truck in here to pave the damned thing over, complete with gutters and a convenient cul-de-sac. But, of course, that would defeat the whole idea of secrecy.

At last he spotted the familiar rusty pickup, where the road seemed to disappear into brush and old-growth forest. At least it confirmed that Tucker was here.

"I'll have to get a load of gravel dumped out here before I come again," Graham said to himself as he eased his belly out from behind the steering wheel. "I wonder if Tucker has any relatives who could spread it, or if I should hire that done too. Damn, forty-five's too old to go traipsing around in the backwoods." Graham was, in fact, fifty-five.

He hefted himself wheezing out of the low-slung Cadillac, closing the door and zapping the locks. Another zap popped the trunk open. Bracing himself along the car's side, Graham struggled over rocks and ruts to get to it. He pulled out his camouflage hunting jacket and shrugged it on, pulling the zipper halfway up over his paunch.

His custom-built deer rifle was one of many in his collection. He caressed its satin-like, hand-carved cherry stock. Even window-dressing had to be of the finest quality on the market when it belonged to Everett Graham. He patted the hunting jacket's chest pocket to be sure his map was there. It was, of course. He liked to be sure of things.

He fished a couple of shells out of another pocket, slid the bolt back and pressed them one at a time into the magazine. He had never actually seen a bear on any of his forays into these god forsaken woods, but Tucker insisted they were there, and it paid to be prepared.

Everett surveyed the open woodland of oak, hickory and locust. If the road ran any further into the trees, it was long since overgrown. Tucker's trail began somewhere in here, and the only way to find it was to know where it started. Graham squinted into the underbrush. White blooms of wild cherry gleamed through the dense shade like a signpost, pointing to the creek. Graham plunged into the thick underbrush. He'd done this plenty of times before.

Spring rains and melting snow had swollen the stream into a boisterous cataract that buffeted and swamped a line of stones across it. Graham scanned the map and then the line of trees on the other side of the creek. No sense stepping into that icy water before he had to. Ahh, there it was. The deer-rub scar on that oak tree. Sure sign of the deer trail he was looking for. He dipped the toe of a well-greased boot into the water like a timid non-swimmer.

Following the trail was easy for about a mile. He stopped suddenly at the sound of a rustle. As he slipped the rifle off his back, he looked around. He hadn't really hunted in years, but the old instincts were still there. He positioned the stock butt against his shoulder, just in case. There, in a thicket, a buck bounded away from him. He slipped off the safety and put the deer in his sights. Just as he was about to squeeze the trigger, he stopped. He'd have to dress the thing and lug it out. It was not deer season. Just too much trouble. This whole trip was that way. Must be getting lazy. He returned his attention to following the trail.

His partner, Tucker, was cagy and secretive, just like all the old Appalachian mountain people who scraped out a living in these hills. Tucker'd rather walk these miles. Wouldn't do this the easy way, on a horse or a dirt bike. No, he had to do like he suspected Tucker's daddy did when he ran a still—always on the watch for someone to do him dirty. Grudgingly, Graham supposed he had the right idea. But it was still a damned pain in the neck.

Everett's roots were here, too, but in town, not back in the woods. Pulling a fast one on Tucker was almost better than winning in the stock market. Out-foxing the fox, so to speak.

Graham had just about enough of those trashy Tuckers. They'd been in this area a long time, like his family, but they were peculiar and cantankerous, keeping to themselves back in the hollers. They were all poor as dirt and stubborn as mules, a trifling, unseemly lot he would never have associated himself with—if it hadn't been for the emerald mine. And even now, his association with them was a closely-guarded secret.

No one knew the source of his vast fortune, not even family. Folks in the area believed he was some kind of stock market genius, and he was pleased to cultivate that illusion. The truth was, ten years ago he had agreed to pay Tucker's back property taxes in return for a share of the mine Tucker had been working on his property. Tucker did all the manual labor, excavating the gems and turning them over to his partner to be sold through a New York agent and the profits invested. It was a good deal for both, as the agreement went.

Of course, it was true that Graham had taken to borrowing from Tucker's share to fund his own ventures and comforts. The way he figured it, Tucker was too busy to notice and really had little need for or appreciation of wealth anyway. Graham, on the other hand, had grown up with means and needed to maintain a certain level of style. Surely a reasonable person would understand that. Anyway, he would correct the books once that Beta Max stock went up and nobody would be the wiser. In truth, Tucker was lucky to have him looking after things.

Everett had been walking for well over an hour when he reached another creek. He'd always hated this part, but there was no way to cross except balancing on the downed locust. Bacon and egg breakfasts at Boone Drug and afternoon deal-making bourbons took a toll on his laid-back body. He put the map in his pocket, slung his rifle over his shoulder, and took a deep breath. The wet bark was slick. He grimaced as he went down on all fours. He'd have to practically hug the damn tree to cross.

Bet Tucker scampered across like a squirrel, hang him. Knees weren't made to balance on. Once across, Everett picked up his pace. He turned and zigzagged up the hill with only four stops to catch his breath. Past the old homestead, across another creek, he braced himself for the last push.

Everett hitched up his creased Carhartts, now covered with dust and tree-slime, and faced the endless climb, huffing and puffing, up a rocky mound. He picked his way up the loose stones left over from Tucker's digging out the mountain to get at the emeralds.

The last batch were clear enough to be valued as highly as stones coming out of Colombia. A little fancy bookkeeping would keep Tucker's share a mite short. As stones crunched beneath his boots, he felt more justified that he'd fudged the numbers. In fact, he felt under-compensated.

"'Bout time you got here," Olin Tucker called. He propped a shovel against the wooden beams framing the mine entrance. He waited there casually, hands in his overall pockets, as Graham gutted out the last of the climb and then bent over, gasping, to catch his breath.

Everett stood at the top of the heap, dusted off his hands and pants, then shook Tucker's paw. "This trip gets harder every year."

"Sure enough. I keep pulling out more of the mountain and dumping it down the side. Sit a spell and catch your breath." The mountaineer sat on a boulder and poured them each a cup of coffee from a battered thermos. They talked about the weather, the mountain form of social talk, before getting down to business.

"I know it's my idea to keep our meetings secret, but this hike in here is tough for me."

Tucker nodded. "It's the onliest way I know to show you how hard I work for my share."

"I'm not in as good a shape as you are." Everett envied Olin's lean and limber body but not the labor required to keep it that way. The dust in Tucker's thick grey eyebrows and on his scraggly beard prompted Everett to rub his hand over his own clean-shaven face. "The accountant's still working on the profit statements. We're both doing fair, but most of it's tied up in stocks and bonds."

"So about how much we got?" Tucker studied Graham's face. "Are we millionaires?"

Everett nodded.

Tucker stood and walked to the edge of the heap of tailings before turning to face him. "Four hundred dollars a month ain't cuttin' it. I want to change our contract." Tucker paced along the edge, rubbing his bristly chin. "Now, you've done a good job investing the rest of my half and I thank ye for upholdin' your end. A million dollars is fine for me. I want to cash out. I'm ready to retire and spend time with my wife and grandson. Lucky's gettin' big now."

Everett froze inside. Trapped. Tucker had every right to his own money. A nightmare of financial transactions played through his head. Their combined assets, all in Everett's name, had been his collateral in all his business deals over the years. He stood and nodded, buying time to think. "I know what you mean. I wish I could spend more time with my granddaughter. Emerald gets prettier every day. When did you want to start wrapping up this operation?"

"The sooner the better. I ain't getting any younger," Tucker looked across the valley with his back to Everett. "There's still emeralds aplenty here. You can go after 'em if you want to. I got all I need."

"Listen to reason, man." Graham heard himself babbling, pleading, with this bumpkin who suddenly threatened to ruin him utterly. "You know I have no talent for physical labor. I'm a businessman. We had a deal, you and I."

Tucker glanced at him then returned his gaze to the valley. "Aw, come on, Everett. You know I held up my end. But I cain't dig forever in this rockpile. I got a grandson that hardly knows his grandpap. And you, don't you want to spend more time with your granddaughter?"

"Sure, sure." Graham wasn't fond of children, but Emerald was a bright little girl and he was rather proud of her. That was entirely beside the point. Or maybe it was the point. This fortune he had built—through his own dear effort, mind you—was her inheritance. Why, you might even say he'd done it all for her sake. He wasn't about to let some son of a moonshiner rob his grandchild of her inheritance. Then the questions from brokers, from his family and from the community rang loudly in Everett's head. There was no way he could pull this off and keep his social and financial standing. He couldn't give up half of his wealth.

He couldn't do it. Pain flashed in his forehead. A blaze of red burned in his eyes. Shaking, he stood and stared at Tucker's back. All his heart registered in that instant was the threat. He'd be found out. He'd have to cash in his part of the stocks at a loss just to cough up half of what Tucker had coming. Time. He needed time for the stocks to recover. *He can't do this to me—to Emerald!*

He closed his eyes to blot out the sight of wiping out his empire. Before he knew it, the rifle was off his shoulder and in his hands. He opened his eyes and raised the sight.

Graham squeezed the trigger.

The jolt to his shoulder registered in his memory to be replayed at odd moments for the rest of his life.

Chapter 1

"*If I live through this*," Emerald Graham vowed, "I'll stay on the bunny slope forever." Pain, intense as a red hot poker, ran through her leg, and her knee throbbed. "Hey!" she squealed and threw up her hands to ward off the icy spray as some bratty kid made a parallel turn just above her.

Skiers plummeted past on the hard-packed snow. Sugar Mountain, North Carolina. Tom Terrific, the black diamond slope. Their looks of annoyance confirmed what her rather spectacular fall and the pain in her left knee already told her. Grandfather was right. It's only worth the risk if you don't get caught.

She'd really gotten caught this time.

She lifted one of her hands off the snow to brace her knee and knew immediately it was a mistake. Gravity was not on her side. The earth moved. Correction, she moved, slid a few inches. Her heart thudded in her chest. She automatically calculated the grade of the slope below her—sixty degrees, if she discounted the big bumps. What were the odds of her getting down this North Carolina mountain in one piece?

"O-o-o-h! N-o-o-o . . ." Sliding and screaming, she went for long seconds down the steep incline. She had nothing to grab on to. Plowing her good heel into the snow as a brake only managed to swing her around backwards.

She slid further, fear gathering in her stomach as her speed increased.

Thwack. Her back slammed into a bump, stopping her descent. Afraid to breathe, afraid to move, she squeezed her eyes shut to keep the tears from escaping.

The bump rumbled, like some deep-voiced person clearing his throat. "Hidy. I'm Lucky Tucker with the Ski Patrol. Kin I help you, ma'am?"

She nodded, keeping her eyes closed.

"What's your name?"

Her eyes flew open and she stared up at the broad shouldered, dark haired man in the red jacket towering over her. "Em," was all she could manage.

"The letter 'M'?"

"No, Sherlock, E-M," she spelled out. "Short for Emerald."

"The jewel of your father's heart, Dr. Watson?" He released his skis and propped them up in the snow beside them.

"More like my grandfather's." Despite the ache in her knee, she warmed to his bantering tone and smiled, then grimaced. "Are you my knight in shining armor?"

"More like Prince Charming in long johns. You hurtin'?" he asked, already taking off his bulky ski gloves and kneeling in the snow beside her.

"It feels like someone's hammering on my kneecap from the inside."

"Did you hit your head?"

When she replied that she wasn't sure, he ran his fingertip firmly back over her scalp.

"Oh."

"Did I hurt you?"

"Uh, no." Actually, as tense as she was from the fall, his massaging fingers sent a shudder of relief down her spine, but she wasn't about to tell him that.

He reached toward her leg, and she flinched. He picked up the ski lying next to her which had automatically released from her boot when she fell.

"Here's the other one," the bratty kid said after side stepping back up the hill. Em mentally retracted the "bratty."

"Thank you," she called as the boy skied away. The pain in her leg subsided a bit.

"First I need to cross these to let other skiers know to avoid us." He sidestepped uphill about twenty feet to jam the two skies into the snow, forming an X, and then returned, already asking questions. "What happened?"

"I think I crossed the ski tips and fell sideways—twisted my knee."

"Did you hear or feel a popping noise?"

"No. Is that good or bad?"

"Good. I want to examine you just to be sure nothing else is wrong."

"Are we playing doctor?" She couldn't help herself; he was so professional, so country and so good-looking. And so poor, she added silently after spying his ski boots held together by duct tape.

"Hum," he said, then asked her to look straight into his eyes. He covered one of her eyes for a moment, then uncovered it. She assumed that her pupil contracted correctly. His eyes were such a deep blue that she couldn't tell if his pupils were dilated, but he certainly didn't seem to be responding to her.

When he repeated the procedure with the other eye, he brushed her forehead with the lightest of touches. Was that just an accident? His gaze traveled over her head and face and Em stared into his deep-set cobalt eyes. A Roman nose dominated his sun-browned square face and firm lips. He looked familiar. Surely they had gone to high school together if he was a local.

Of course, Em took all the advanced courses while he was likely in the auto shop. For just a moment she was back in high school hugging her books to her chest hurrying past the hallway of the vocational classes, past the hooded eyes of the country boys leaning against the wall smoking. Had he been one of those?

"Do you like what you see?" she asked. Bravado had always been her defense of choice. She shook her head. It had been too long since her last date.

"Uh huh. No evident damage."

"I told you that. It's my knee that's hurt."

He palpated her leg from the hip to the ankle, giving extra gentle attention to the area around her knee. Even through the ski pants, his probing fingers heightened her senses.

His next questions were all business, designed, she was sure, to set her at ease. His movements were efficient, distant and professional without a hint of impropriety. So why did the places on her body tingle with the familiarity of a lover's touch after he had checked them? This was ridiculous! She would accept the next blind date some over-zealous colleague offered her.

"Feel this?" he asked as he tapped on the bottom of her boot.

"Yes, but I don't think I can straighten my leg."

"Can you wiggle your toes?"

Happy that her foot, at least, was in working order, she replied. "Yes. Does this mean I'll live?"

"If you behave yourself and do exactly what I say." He pulled out a pair of scissors.

She sucked in her breath. "Uh, can we not do that?" She looked away, a little embarrassed. "These ski pants are Bogners. I picked the color to match my eyes." Until recently, she'd never had to be concerned with money since the estate's accountant took care of paying all the bills. "And really . . . my knee is already feeling better."

"Well, I guess blood would show up pretty well on that bright green, and you don't seem to have a broken bone," he said, replacing the scissors in his pack. "A more thorough exam can wait."

"Thanks for the good news." Stiff from sitting, she knew she would creak if she moved. The packed snow froze her backside, the cold seeped up her body despite the expensive padding.

He called on his radio for a rescue sled. Just then, three men skied up and stopped.

"Hey, Cuz, you need any help?"

Lucky glanced their way. "Not your kind. I'm still suffering from your last visit. Go on. Git. Let me work in peace. This lady don't need any of your kind of attention."

"Grady here's only got a few days leave from the army. Are you goin' to treat your kin that way?"

Lucky sighed. "Em, these three ya-hoos are my cousins. They spent the night at my house. Grady's the stiff one, comes from 'yes sirrin' those officers. Clayton and Wes are local. Wes got married not long ago, so he's tamed down some."

"Think I can trust Lucky with my knee?" Em smiled at each of the men.

"Medically? Yeah. Otherwise, it's hard to say." Wes grinned then nodded to Lucky. "Thanks for last night. This is our last run. 'Til next time." The three swooshed away in perfect form.

"Do that again and I'm pulling your ticket!" Lucky yelled after them.

"Back to business," Lucky said, shaking his head. "Why did you try Tom Terrific? It's one of the toughest slopes."

"Brilliant scholar that I am, I believed George when he said skiing is easy. He told me to take a left at the top of the mountain and to point those skis down the hill and let gravity do its thing. I have conditioned on a ski machine." At his knowing smile, she added, "You've heard this story before."

"You'd be amazed at the number of times. Is your boyfriend here today?"

"He's not my boyfriend, or even my friend after this. We're merely colleagues." Em shivered. "How much longer do we have to wait?"

"Another patroller's bringing the sled. Where's your hat?"

"I didn't wear one. It would mess up my hair." At the telltale shake of his head, she added, "Another common mistake, I take it."

At the moment he nodded, a skier stopped near them. "Doctor Graham, are you okay?"

"I'm in capable hands, Kevin. Thanks for asking."

As he skied away, Lucky asked, "Medical?"

When she shook her head, he returned to the business at hand. She knew PhDs were a dime a dozen in this college town.

"We'll put a temporary splint on your knee, strap you in the sled, and take you down to the ski patrol first aid building. Get set for a few bumps on the ride."

"What? You don't have fluffy cushions in the sled to protect this fragile body?"

"No ma'am." Another red-jacketed patroller snowboarded down in front of a long, low, red metal sled. "Our main concern is to get you down quickly and safely."

"Lucky me," she murmured.

"I'm Lucky, you're Em. Remember?" He smiled at her before turning to brief the other patroller.

Em stared up at the dark-haired man who had rescued her. His eyes matched the clear, crisp, deep blue early January sky behind him. It might be interesting to get to know him better. So what if he was broke and local? He couldn't be worse than some of the blind dates she'd been on.

"We'll be as gentle as possible," he said, maneuvering a hinged padded splint on both sides of her left leg. "Your carriage awaits, milady, but we'll need your help getting you into it. Dean, my boss here, will lift your injured leg, and I'll grip under your shoulders and lift the rest of you. You'll have to hop up on your good leg."

"But I'll be facing uphill," she said, disturbed at the thought of not being able to see where she was going. That sensation had already happened to her once today.

He nodded. "The leg goes uphill to minimize further injury. Are you ready? On the count of three: one—two—three."

"You two have done this before," Emerald said as a way of complimenting the men as they laid her back and positioned Lucky's medical fanny pack under her head. They covered her with a blanket, placed her skis and poles beside her, and fastened her in with three straps. Before she could think of anything else to say, she whizzed backward down the slope at a much faster speed than she'd been willing, much less able, to ski.

"Whoa boy, whoa boy," she said, more to calm herself than to actually tell the men how to get her off the mountain. Bundled up skiers stared down at her as she passed them. The swirling wind tugged at her hair. Faster and faster she went, feeling only slight bumping through the cold metal shell. Some carriage, she thought, as her fingers curled into knots to control the terror of flying backwards. People appeared in her peripheral vision then swiftly shrank to the size of miniature dolls. Dean kept the rope taut behind the tail of the sled, snowboarding as though he'd been born to it.

She could hear Lucky's skis cutting through the hard-packed snow when he turned, and she relaxed. They knew what they were doing. It reminded her of the sleigh rides she had taken at college in Canada, only she had faced the direction they headed, and the horses responded when she called "whoa."

The ride ended at the bottom of the beginners' area—easy to spot with so many people falling down. "Thank you, kind sir, for the ride," she said as Lucky loosened the restraining straps.

"My pleasure. To get you out of your carriage, we'll reverse the process and put you into this chair to wheel you inside. Ready?"

"Whoa! State of the art medical equipment?" Em stared doubtfully at what looked like a straight chair strapped to a hand truck like delivery men used.

"A regular wheel chair isn't maneuverable enough in these conditions. You'll be fine; just lean back and pretend you're a UPS package."

With his help, Emerald sat up, then awkwardly stepped on her good leg and fell into the chair. They paused inside the door. The walls were unpainted wood; the room was clean but well-used. Lucky wheeled her to a bed at the back of the long room and steadied her as she hopped aboard. None of the other eight beds were occupied; Em guessed nobody else had been stupid enough to get hurt yet that day.

The fluorescent lights were unforgiving, highlighting the wet boot tracks on the industrial carpet beneath the chair wheels. Medical supplies lined the inside of a cabinet a patroller just opened. A white-haired woman sat at a desk discussing a form with another patroller.

"Is this normal?" she asked, indicating the empty beds.

"Sort of. Most accidents happen between three to four in the afternoon when the light goes flat. People are tired, but too caught up to stop skiing for the day. 'Course, a few have a couple of beers for the afternoon runs."

She felt better already. She shucked out of her ski jacket and draped it over the bottom of the cot.

"To keep that knee from swelling, we'll put an ice pack on it."

After she lay back in the bed with her splinted knee covered in ice, Lucky grabbed a clipboard and sat in the wooden chair beside her. "Do you want me to have this George guy paged?"

She shook her head. "I'm in my own car."

"OK, I have a few questions to ask you. . . ."

The questions ranged from address and telephone number to how many falls she'd had that day. The pain in her knee was almost gone. She eventually interrupted him with, "May I have a cup of coffee? I'm feeling much better now."

"We can only offer water in the patient area."

"Could we go somewhere else and finish with your questions? I'd love to buy you a cup of coffee. It's the least I can do." Now that she was safe and warm, she needed a pick-me-up.

"Our services are free, but we do take donations to cover supplies." He pointed to a miniature foot cast with a dollar sign crudely drawn on it. But there was a twinkle in his eyes, and she knew he'd deliberately misunderstood her invitation.

"Let me put it another way—I need a cup of coffee. Caffeine. The stronger the better. Where can we go?"

"What about your knee?"

"It doesn't hurt anymore. I'll prove it. Take off the splint and let me give it a try," she insisted over his protest. After he unbuckled the splint, she sat up and lowered her legs over the side of the bed.

Lucky grasped her upper arms to support her. "You should have your doctor examine that knee."

"I will, I promise. See?" she said as she stood up and straightened her leg. She held her breath, afraid her bravado had betrayed her once again, but, remarkably, the knee did feel almost okay. "It's much better. Your healing fingers must have done the trick." When he released his firm grasp of her arms, she was almost sorry she had spoken so quickly. She straightened and tested her weight on the leg. It was stiff and sore, but the throbbing was gone.

With a tight hold on Lucky's arm, Em limped out of the patient area and into the ski patroller break room where the aroma of fresh brewed coffee greeted her. A mild locker room smell mixed with burnt toast lingered. Half eaten cake sat on one of the two tables. A handwritten notice was taped to the refrigerator "Thou shall not covet thy neighbor's food !!!."

Double racks of skis ran the length of the opposite wall. Boot heaters were plugged in at different points, some with boots attached. A blackboard listed initials and lunch break times for the day. A big sign stated no use of cell phones while working. Another one said "Take things home with you. Pearle has been known to donate heavily to RAM's Rack."

"'Mountain three, patrollers zero.' What does that mean?"

Lucky glanced at the blackboard and shrugged. "Three of the pros have been hurt this year, and so far, the mountain is still undamaged."

"That's encouraging."

Chapter 2

Lucky filled his favorite cup and a Styrofoam one for Emerald. "Cream and sugar?" he asked over his shoulder, then put a little of both in his.

"No, I'll take it straight."

He handed her the coffee, and said, "I'll be right back, I need to tell Pearle we'll be in here."

The sweet-faced white haired woman smiled as he approached. "Taking a break?"

"She requested coffee. I'm just obliging a patient. Emerald's knee seems fine but we need to finish filling out your forms for you."

"Emerald, is it? Is that really her name, or are you just dazzled by that classy green outfit?" Pearle's eyes twinkled. "Do her eyes match?"

"As a matter of fact, they do."

Pearle chuckled. "The state appreciates your dedication in getting those forms filled out. Take your time; be thorough."

"Yes, ma'am." As Lucky walked back the long aisle to the break room, he admitted to himself that his interest in Em went beyond the normal patient-rescuer relationship. She was totally out of his class, of course. The Graham's department store was an old Boone landmark. The old store closed years ago, but the Graham name was always in the paper connected with some big gift to the university, so the family still had money from somewhere. Bet she didn't have to worry about her grandma's back property taxes.

It was only a cup of coffee.

Lucky paused in the doorway, struck by the gleam of her wavy auburn hair in the light. He'd seen that apple-cider colored hair before . . . from the back of calculus class his senior year in high school. The Graham girl. She'd been a bright sophomore on the front row. It had to be her.

"So, what do you do when you're not rescuing damsels in distress?" Em asked as he sat down.

"You mean, what's my real job?"

"If you wish. You do look a bit old to be playing on a mountain all day."

"I'm only thirty. Not much older than you."

At her exaggerated frown, he continued, "I'll have you know, we who *play* are highly-trained professionals who take extensive courses in Winter Emergency Care as well as skiing."

"I merely meant that most people our age have *real* jobs. Getting paid to ski is in the same category as lifeguarding—something college students do before getting on with life." Em frowned and glanced away. "Am I digging a deep hole here? I sound like some kind of job-snob. Sometimes I speak before thinking. No offense meant."

"None taken." He pulled his lips together to keep his smile in check. Obviously, she wasn't badly hurt and could be released from his care. "Skiing's a hard job but somebody has to do it."

"You poor man. Do you get hazardous-duty pay?"

A white-bearded patroller clomped by at that moment and answered. "Hazardous-Duty Pay? We'll have to take that up with management."

Lucky grinned. "Em, meet Lyle—one of our longtime patrollers. Is he too old to get paid to play?"

Em's face turned red.

"Be good to our resident Santa Claus or there'll be nothing under your tree next Christmas." Lyle nodded in agreement to Lucky's warning, then winked and left.

"I guess we'd better finish up this form." Lucky said and took a sip of his coffee.

"Is that a photo of your dog?" Em asked, gazing at the cup.

"That's Hambone. He's bigger than you—165 pounds of husky-chow mix. His eyes are a beautiful shade of green." He paused and looked at his coffee cup, then back at Em. "Just like yours."

Emerald let loose a laugh that sounded as if it started down in her belly, bubbled up and escaped out of her fast-talking mouth. "Why you silver-tongued devil, you!"

Lucky grinned. He was on a roll. "Your hair's the color of apple cider vinegar—the kind you squirt on a passel of collard greens. And your cheeks are as smooth . . . as ripe, juicy South Carolina peaches." His voice dropped on the last word and his mouth went dry as her laughter stopped and her cheeks glowed.

Lucky took a swallow of the now-cooled coffee and leveled an evaluating gaze at the woman before him. Normally, a patient was a patient, nothing more. He rescued them, fixed them up, filled out the paperwork, and then turned them over to loved ones or the hospital. But this woman was different. She made him want to laugh at odd moments. She'd even managed to flirt with him while suffering with a newly twisted knee. She had guts, he had to admit that.

"How's the knee?" he asked as he set down his coffee cup and picked up the pen attached by cord to the clipboard.

"Fine. I'll be able to limp out of here under my own power."

He'd seen others do the same before without long-term injury. "Before you go, I need you to sign this form."

She reached for the pen and accidently knocked his cup. Neither of them had time to react before it slid to the edge of the table and dropped off. He jerked back. The cup landed in his lap. Coffee sloshed all over the front of the white ski sweater, a Christmas gift from his grandmother.

"Oh, no! I'm so sorry." Emerald jumped up, then grimaced. Upon hearing her swift intake of breath, his own knee twinged in sympathy. She yanked paper towels off the metal holder and tried to wipe the liquid off the black radio harness strapped across his chest. The dark stain seeped into the white close-knit sweater. She dabbed the paper on his abdomen to no avail. She leaned over him and frowned.

"I believe you," he said, taking her hand in his. When she raised her eyes to look into his, her lips were only inches away and time lost all meaning for Lucky. Her frown softened into a surprised "oh." Each of the long lashes surrounding her eyes became distinct to him as he remained spellbound in her gaze.

"Thirty to twenty-one," squawked the radio on his chest, effectively snapping him to alert.

Lucky released her hand. "Go ahead, thirty."

"Could you put up some hazard poles at tower twenty-two on yellow? Skiers are creating a jump, and it's too congested there."

"Ten-four."

"I'll have that sweater dry cleaned for you," Em said quickly. "Do you have something else you could put on?"

Rather than argue since he had to get back to work, Lucky agreed. He retrieved an old gray sweater from his locker, unclipped his radio harness and laid it on the table. As he skinned out of the white sweater, the thermal undershirt stuck to it and came off too. "Drat!" Static crackled from the wool sweater, making his chest hair snap to attention. He rubbed it down and put his thermal back on along with the dry sweater.

Em was poised with the pen over the report.

"Did you sign that yet?"

"Uh, sure." Em hastily scribbled her name and handed him the form. "Do you have a number so I can reach you when this is cleaned?"

He took a business card from his locker and handed it to her. "The second number is my home phone."

"So you do have a real job!"

"Custom blinds and closet reorganization is limited to weekend work during ski season. I get busy in the summer. I've got to run. Have a doctor look at that knee," were his last words as he headed back to the slopes.

~

Five days after meeting Emerald, and Lucky still couldn't get the woman off his mind. He settled in for an evening with Hambone in front of the fire with the latest issue of *Ski Patrol* magazine. The day had been brutally cold and he'd brought in a record number of skiers with possible frostbite. The warmth of the fire seeped into his bones, taking the chill out of his fingers and toes. His frenzied thoughts calmed to match the quiet in the room.

When the telephone rang, he almost didn't answer it, but realized it could be a closet job. He was running out of options on raising thousands quickly to help his grandma out of this bind. Wish she had let him know of her problems last summer instead of being so stubborn and proud. He could have postponed adding the deck to his house. He could have taken on more jobs and worked seven days for a while. Taxes and knees. A double whammy. Triple, since she said it was both legs botherin' her.

"Lucky here," he said into the mouthpiece.

"This is Emerald Graham, the one who spilled coffee on your sweater last Wednesday."

Lucky became aware of the sound of his heart beating. "How's the knee?" he asked and leaned back into his well-worn recliner.

"It worked fine the next morning, but I did as you insisted and saw the doctor. No damage. As a matter of fact, I plan to ski Wednesday afternoon. Will you be there?"

"I'm there five days a week, in snow, sleet or hail. Push comes to shove, I'm even there in the rain but under protest."

"You and the mail carriers are all dedicated to duty. But seriously, I'd like to return your sweater."

"I'll meet you in the patrol room at one, that's my lunch break. Are you taking a lesson this time?"

She laughed. "I have a private lesson scheduled at two. I was hoping to take a run with you later to show my progress."

"I'll find you on the beginners' slope. You were wearing a green outfit, right?"

"Yes. I bought it to match my skis."

"Thought it matched your eyes."

"Yes, well, I wear a lot of green."

Lucky cringed—a ski slope clothes hound, just the type he needed to be attracted to. Her outfit would have cost him a few months' pay and she spent it like it was small change. He couldn't play in her league. Too bad, because she intrigued him. "You look prettier than a pole-cat in it."

"Do you think so? I could use the emotional boost after my last episode."

"Most people would have given up after a first experience like that. Why aren't you?"

"This is my year to ski. Last year I took up climbing, the year before was biking, the year before that was karate."

"What brought all this on, if you don't mind my getting personal?"

"Only if I can ask you a question . . ."

The magazine Lucky'd been holding slid from his fingers and landed on Hambone's head. Hambone growled and started to rip the magazine apart. "No!" Lucky commanded.

"No? I'm sorry that I bothered you," she said stiffly.

"Not you. I was talking to the dog."

Hambone regained his composure, yawned and lay down at Lucky's feet.

Emeralds in the Snow

"The one with eyes like mine?"

"You remembered."

"I've never had a dog . . . or any pet, for that matter."

"A house without a pet is like a flower garden without birds—it might look right, but something vital's missing." Lucky leaned to Hambone and said softly, "How about a scratch behind the ears?"

"Well, if you think I'll like it."

"Like what?" Lucky absently scratched the dog.

"A scratch behind the ears."

Lucky chuckled, thinking he might like it himself. "I was talking to the dog."

"You could be right. I wonder how my mother'd feel about having a dog or cat in the house."

"You live with your parents?" Lucky settled back in the chair and luxuriated in the sound of her voice.

"My mother's all the family I have left. My grandfather passed away last summer, and Mother was all alone in this big place so I decided to join her. She's shy. If it weren't for me, the housekeeper would be the only person she'd talk to."

"Family ranks number one in my book. Where were you before?"

"Arizona. I went to college in Canada, and got a doctorate in math at Vanderbilt."

"You've got a whole passle of letters after your name."

"I worked for them, believe me. When my grandfather had a stroke, I applied to teach at Appalachian State so I could move back to Boone."

"ASU's a good school. All I've got is a high school diploma and a bunch of emergency medical training certificates." His gut tightened at the glaring differences between them. "But I know more about finding 'sang than you'll ever want to know."

"Ginseng? I might want to spend a spring day with you looking for it."

What am I getting myself into, he thought. She's booking my spring calendar. "We could do that, but it's harvested in the fall and a 'sanger never reveals locations. I've known of people who have stolen plants from front yards. Some people are greedy, you know? No matter how much they have, they want more. With 'sang, they take all of it instead of selective harvesting. If people aren't careful, they'll pull up all the plants and then no one'll have any. You need to take a little and leave a little, like most things in this life." He paused, then added, "I didn't mean to get on my high horse about that."

"I understand. I believe in holding onto things that are special to me, too."

"Like what?"

"Promise you won't laugh?"

"I'll try." He expected her to mention a porcelain collection or a favorite doll.

"Emeralds."

"Emeralds?" he repeated. "I never would have guessed." Big money, he thought, remembering that he'd broken his last ten to buy dog food.

"It's become a passion with me."

His heart thudded in his chest when she said *passion*.

"I have a collection of gem quality emeralds still in matrix that I picked up at rock shows. They're more interesting than the ones already faceted you buy from a jeweler. Plus some raw emeralds my grandfather gave me for special occasions. There are markers in the stone that can identify which country the stone came from, even which mine."

"I never knew that. I guess it makes sense that you collect them. Pearle, the lady that runs the ski patrol room, collects pearls—says her mother did too. Did your mother collect emeralds?"

She laughed. "My grandfather insisted on the name, and that was before my eyes proved to be green."

"Back to my first question, why a new sport each year?"

"It beats being trapped in a gym. A man I dated in college was an avid swimmer and he got me started. Later, I met somebody who was a karate expert, and I've continued with other sports on my own since then."

"Since you're from Boone, I'm surprised you didn't ski before now." He heard her take a deep breath before answering.

"Grandfather wouldn't let me—it was too risky. My father was killed out west by an avalanche when I was seven."

Lucky paused, visualizing a girl lost without her father. "I know what that's like. My dad died when I was young, too. How did it happen?"

"He and two friends were skiing out of bounds. My grandfather refused to let me ski and I didn't question it. Mother and I moved in with him after my father's death, and his word was law in that household. It wasn't so bad since I was away at boarding school my junior and senior years of high school."

"So skiing is much more than just another sport to you."

"Uh-huh, but the accident happened over twenty years ago. I'm not about to do anything out of bounds."

"I'll pull your lift ticket if you do," Lucky said, half in jest, to lighten the mood.

"I'll behave, at least until I'm a good skier. What happened to your dad?"

"He turned over a tractor when I was ten. Mom couldn't handle it up here without him. After a few years, she went home to Charlotte and left me with my grandparents. She remarried a little later. I don't see her much."

"How did they meet?"

Lucky sighed. "Dad worked for a while at the university maintenance department. He saw her one day on campus and asked her out. They didn't have much in common. But those were still the days of free love. I was a surprise so they got married."

"Do you want to talk about this?"

"Not really."

"Good. Let's move on. The closets in this house are a mess. Would you be interested in redoing them for me?"

"I'll be glad to give you an estimate and then you can make up your mind."

"Could you come over tomorrow after you finished skiing for the day? The housekeeper's a wonderful cook and she could set another place at the table."

"That's not necessary," he said hurriedly. She moved fast, maybe a little too fast for him. "I'll grab something on the way over and meet you later, say seven o'clock. Is that too early?"

"That's fine." After jotting down her address in the ritzy section on Howard's Knob, he hung up the phone.

The fire had died down. He ambled over to poke it back to life. Emerald had done that to him, too, stirred him up and ignited thoughts of possibilities. So what if she was rich and educated? Owning things didn't make or break a person. The real test was how you treated your family.

The money from this job could go a long way in paying Grandma's property taxes, but wouldn't help with the double knee operation. Medicare only paid so much, and none of the Tuckers ever had health insurance.

Sometimes the rich were the slowest to pay. Wonder if Em's in that category?

Chapter 3

Lucky expertly eased his old Explorer into the tight curve and accelerated up the steep hill. High Point Drive offered a panoramic view of the picturesque downtown and ASU in Boone. But the view came with a price. Most homes sported at least one monster four-wheel-drive vehicle in their driveways.

Em's house was unmistakable from her description. Lights blazed in the yard and in the three large dormers topped with half-moon glass windows. Such a multi-peaked roof was expensive to build, Lucky thought. A brick drive circled in front of the three car garage that took up the smaller wing of the house. Within the circle, terraced rows of trimmed rose bushes hinted at summer glory. All first class. As Lucky carefully wiped his shoes on the mat, he noticed the signature corner piece of a well-known local artist in the stained glass of the double doors. A trim woman in her fifties answered the door.

"Mrs. Graham?"

A polite smile greeted him. "No, I'm the housekeeper, Martha. You must be Lucky. Lynette and Emerald are in the living room. Follow me, please."

The crab orchard stone floor in the foyer led to a two-story open area. The walls over the wide stairs held paintings that looked old and expensive, judging by the ornate wood of the frames. Five years of building his own house had taught Lucky a thing or two about construction and wood. Then too, he had been in many of the expensive homes in Boone and knew their closets intimately.

Em spoke as soon as he entered the living room. "Mother, this is Lucky. Lucky, my mother, Lynette Graham." The woman offered her hand but kept her eyes downcast.

"It's nice to meet you, Mrs. Graham." Lucky took her fingertips gently, very aware of the callouses on his own. He searched for something to put her at ease. "Did I see evidence of a rose garden?"

"Why, yes, Lucky." She looked up at him for the first time. "Do you like flowers?"

"My Grandma swears she can't live without them. She tends to them as closely as she does the vegetables. Do you have a place for wild flowers, too?"

She nodded and smiled the sweetest little smile he'd ever seen. "It's near the woods to the right of the house and continues in the back."

Lucky winked at Emerald before returning his attention to the woman in front of him. It was like coaxing a deer. "I know of an old logging road that's choked full of trillium just begging to be put somewhere to be better appreciated. You can't have too many of those. I'll get you some after they bloom in the spring."

"That's very kind of you."

"I'd be happy to do it." Lucky turned his attention to Em. "Which closets were you thinking about changing?"

"I thought we'd start in my grandfather's room. I'll show you."

Lucky followed Em up the curving staircase placing his feet precisely so as not to mark the creamy carpeting. The hand rail looked like walnut, and he bet it really was—not just stained maple—the eight inch crown moldings, too. Em's family must have money to burn.

As she led him upstairs, she warned, "This room is still set up to take care of a sick man. We haven't gotten around to doing anything with it."

"If you want to give it away. . ." he began as they entered the large room, complete with a fireplace and a bank of floor-to-ceiling windows. "Good grief, woman, you've got enough equipment in here to furnish a hospital emergency room and a physical therapy office."

"I was out West when Grandfather had his stroke so Mother bought anything that the doctors mentioned. She took care of him for the last six months. He was doing okay—Mother was happy to be needed—and then his heart just stopped beating."

"I'm sorry for you and your mother."

"Thank you. But my concern now is Mother. She hasn't found anything but gardening to interest her since then."

Lucky walked around the hospital bed and pushed a button that silently raised the head. "So she liked taking care of her father-in-law when he was sick?"

Em nodded. "In case you couldn't tell, she's shy. All that dropped away when she was feeding him, helping him get up or get dressed, even listening to him rant and rave about the after-effects of the stroke. I think she blossomed because she was needed."

Lucky hesitated. "I know I'm poking my nose in someone else's business, but the hospital needs volunteers. Would you mind if I suggest it to her?"

"Not at all, but don't be surprised if she refuses. Meeting new people frightens her."

"Leave it to me." The hospital would win and so would Lynette. He loved neat, practical solutions.

"The closet's over here. We've already boxed up Grandfather's clothes," Em walked to the far end of the room and pulled the double doors wide.

"You don't have any family skeletons in here, do you?"

"Not even an old dog bone. Well, we've never had a dog."

Lucky flipped on the light switch and measured the closet, then had Em show him those in the other bedrooms. When they walked into her bedroom, Lucky was struck by how much warmer and more inviting her room was than any of the others he'd seen. "Is that a fainting couch?"

She nodded. "It's my favorite spot for reading and swooning when I get scratched behind the ears."

"In your Bogner's?"

"Forget I mentioned the Bogners. I don't want you to think I'm just a debutante when you clearly work so hard."

"So, no more ski pants or ear scratching remarks?"

Em just groaned.

The sleigh bed was covered with a green comforter, probably imported from Europe. The dressers and desk didn't look like they came from High Point either. Even though the furniture capital of America was right down the road, she had to buy from another country. But the room felt right, felt inviting. "Did you decorate this yourself?"

"How could you tell?"

"It's cozy." And smells like you, he added silently. That hint of roses.

"Thank you."

"Any secret dreams tucked away in the closet?"

Em smiled. "You might find a stray Barbie doll; the rest of the collection is stored in the attic."

"When you played house," he asked standing close to her, "what did the husband look like?"

"Tall, dark and handsome, of course." She looked up at him.

Good, he thought. He fit the tall and dark part. "Did the house look like this one?"

"Oh, no. It was a rustic Craftsman-style house with dark red walls and a steep-shingled roof. It was in the woods and nature took care of the yard." As she spoke, her hands shaped the house and her outstretched arms indicated the yard area.

He stared down at her for a long moment. Her play house description sounded just like the house he'd been building. "How do you remember it so well?"

She shrugged. "When you're an only child, you learn to make your own entertainment. I had books I read over and over. And I had favorite scripts I made up for playing with the dolls. One was about a big snowstorm. My play husband and I would slide down the roof. Silly, wasn't it?"

Lucky refrained from brushing a stray curl back from her face. "Not at all. It's just that my life was very different from yours. We mostly played outside. I have a passel o' cousins and my grandma couldn't keep her sanity with all of us indoors."

"Do they all live around here?"

"Boone and Banner Elk. I have more aunts, uncles and cousins than I can count. You should see it when we all get together on Grandma's birthday at her place. Fifty or sixty relatives usually show up."

"A real family reunion."

Unsure how to react to the wistfulness in her voice, Lucky nodded and walked to her bedroom walk-in closet. Time to get to work. He measured it and asked her a few questions about how she wanted to use it differently. He didn't know fashion, but the dresses looked well-made and the suits looked finer than any he'd ever owned. And shoes? She had more shoes stacked neatly on the floor than he had tools in his workshop.

"We could put tilt-out shoe racks on this side or a column of short shelves over here."

"Why don't you draw them up both ways and then I'll decide?"

He nodded. "We're finished in here. Do you want me to take a look at improving storage space in the pantry and other areas in the kitchen?"

"All this and windows too. You do know how to make a woman happy."

"I aim to please." When they went to the kitchen, he found that the housekeeper had not yet retired for the evening. Lucky discussed changes with her before following Em into the living room.

"I'm going to have a glass of wine. Would you join me?"

Lucky hesitated. Wine was never one of his favorites.

"We have beer if you prefer."

"You do?"

"There are times when nothing but a cold beer will do," Em said loftily.

"Spoken like a true brew drinker. I'd like one, then I need to head back home. I want to start entering some of these numbers into the computer."

"There's a program for this?"

"I've adapted one to my needs." She handed him a Moosehead and he shook his head, refusing an offer of a glass. "Did you develop a taste for this while you were in Canada?" he asked when she sat next to him on the navy leather couch.

"That and nachos. Our Friday night rituals also included high decibel music in smoke-filled rooms. You know, the regular college thing."

"I never went to college, remember?" he said.

"Sorry. I forgot. You're so easy to talk to I keep thinking . . . Never mind. I'm only making it worse."

"Not everyone who's smart, goes to college," he said a bit too quickly.

"And vice versa," she said and clinked her wine glass against his beer bottle. "You don't think I'm a snob, do you?"

"How am I supposed to answer that loaded question? If I say 'no,' you'll be relieved but wonder if I'm just being nice. If

I say 'yes,' you'll be hurt and want specifics. So I'll plead the fifth and say 'no comment.'"

"Talk about boosting my ego. One minute you gaze into my eyes and send shivers of anticipation down my spine, and the next minute you're pushing me away."

There was more than a touch of truth to her teasing. Lucky looked down at the beer in his hand. "Let's just say that I'm attracted to you but have no business being so." He looked straight at her. "For a number of reasons, you and I wouldn't work out in the long run. And frankly, I'm past the stage of playing the field or whatever they call it now. I don't have the time or energy to invest in someone whose only interest in me is because she has time on her hands and wants to play around."

Em blanched, and Lucky cringed. Maybe he'd read her wrong.

"I don't know who you're talking about because that doesn't describe me. I'm the same age you are," she said, poking him in the chest with her finger, "and I value myself too much to 'play around' with just anyone!" Eyes blazing, she crossed her arms over her chest.

"Ouch, I deserved that." His overreaction had stirred up a hornet's nest. Lucky held out his hand for her to shake. "Truce?"

She paused a long time. "You don't deserve it but okay." She shook his hand and held it for a moment and asked, "So, are you interested in me?"

He gently squeezed her fingers. "I shouldn't be. Let's leave it at that for now." He released her hand and stood. "Do you think your mother's handy? I'd like to talk to her about the hospital work."

"She's probably in the library."

Two of the library walls were completely covered with shelves full of books, many leather-bound. A large table occupied the center of the room. Floor lamps stood next to leather chairs in the four corners of the room.

"Em tells me you did a wonderful job of taking care of your father-in-law after his stroke." Lucky genuinely liked the quiet woman before him.

She blushed at her daughter's compliment. "I did my best."

"My uncle's always talking about needing more help at Watauga Medical Center. He's a volunteer and carts prescriptions around two days a week. I'd like to introduce you to him, if you'd a mind to. He says they're desperate for someone to work with those babies that are born early, the preemies."

"I don't know." Doubt clouded Lynette's eyes.

"At least talk to him," he coaxed. "Or you could deliver flowers to the patients and read to some of them if helping with the babies doesn't interest you."

"Those babies are so tiny."

"And they need someone to give them back rubs while they're in incubators."

"What if I hurt one?"

He had her! "The nurses will show you what to do and be nearby if you need them. Your touch would make a big difference to those babies."

She frowned and Lucky's confidence dropped. Her next words surprised him. "I won't make any promises, but I will meet your uncle."

"Great! He'll be there Thursday. I could meet you at the hospital at four. Is that too late for you?"

"That will be fine."

"He'll be happier than a cat basking in the sun. See you then."

Em walked him to the front door where she retrieved his coat from the foyer closet and held it up for him to put on. "I can't believe you persuaded Mother to actually meet a stranger and then to be among people she doesn't know. She's been painfully shy for so long."

"Maybe she's ready for a change. Don't worry, I'll take good care of her." Lucky put on his gloves.

"Thank you," Em said as she put on her own coat. "I'll walk you to your truck."

"It's fifteen degrees out there. You don't need to do that."

Em hooked her arm through his and opened the door. "Don't tell me what I need to do. I'm a big girl now with my own agenda. Besides, the cold doesn't bother me."

"I admit that I feel honored having a lady walk me to my truck. Do you do this often?"

She laughed. "No, this is my first time." When he reached for the truck door, she stopped him with a hand on his. "Would you mind if I kissed you?" she asked, chin tilted up, her eyes half-closed and alluring.

"Another first for you?"

"Not my first kiss but my first time asking for one. How am I doing?"

He lowered his head to hers in answer. Her lips were warm in contrast to his own. He pulled her closer and deepened the kiss and ceased to think but only to feel. A mix of the comfort of home with the searing heat of being too close to the fire enveloped him.

What was she doing? His befuddled mind finally realized that she was pulling away. The kiss had to end. Reluctantly, he tamped down his passion and tapered off to a kiss at one corner of her lips, then one on the other, and followed it with a deep, heart-felt sigh.

"I meant that to be a sweet 'thank you' kiss," she said, an ironic smile tugging at the corners of her mouth.

"I can't wait to see what I get for skiing with you tomorrow."

"If you can *see* the kiss, that means you kiss with your eyes open."

Lucky had to laugh. He rubbed his hands up and down the arms of her coat, reluctant to end their time together, knowing all the while that he had to leave. "I never thought I'd say this to anyone, but I'm glad you fell at the top of the mountain the other day."

"So am I."

"Until tomorrow, milady," he said, bowed slightly, got into the truck, and watched her in his rearview mirror until he rounded the curve. If wishes were dollar bills, he'd be rich as she was. As it was, she was out of his reach. For the first time in his life, he wished his grandpa had left him a fortune instead of two hundred acres in the next county. After a moment of contemplating, he took back the wish. He was happy with his own legacy.

Chapter 4

Emerald stood outside the Ski Patrol building at a quarter to one the next afternoon and scanned the slopes for the tall, red-jacketed man who'd stolen a kiss from her the night before—and stolen it was. Semi-stolen, she corrected herself, for she had been uncharacteristically bold in asking for it.

Was she reading too much into the kiss? She didn't think so. Just the memory made her heart beat faster and her stomach quiver. With closed eyes, she licked her lower lip and willed him to come to her. She squeezed his cleaned sweater tightly to her and repeated his name over and over. She didn't want to wait any longer to see him.

As a test, she opened one eye to peek out. Lucky stood before her and her mouth dropped open. "Where did you come from?"

"Your dreams?"

"You wish. I didn't hear you ski up."

"I came out of the office behind you. I'd just finished with a report on an earlier accident when I saw you walk up. Nice outfit. Great boots."

"Thank you." She hadn't even considered that he wouldn't be on the slopes. "Here's your sweater."

"I appreciate it. Want a few pointers before your lesson? You'll get more for your money."

"Sure. Lead the way."

Lucky put the sweater in his locker, then showed her the easiest way to carry her skis over her shoulder with tails in front and angled down to avoid hitting anyone behind her. By the time they hiked up the training slope, she was eager to begin. He explained about the step-in bindings she'd purchased, but she couldn't get them to work right. Lucky went down on his knees at her feet and maneuvered her boot onto the ski. She put her hand on his shoulder for balance.

"Every time I see you, you're bowing down to me. First to rescue me, second to measure my closets, and now this. I prefer to have you on my level, kind sir."

Lucky stood. "Which level, milady? The one where I'm five inches taller than you or the one you'll be at if you don't pay attention."

"Equal in spirit, not stature. You know what I mean." The moment of truth had arrived, she had to ski. Her grandfather had forbidden it; her mother was terrified of it, and she'd tried once and failed. This time, she'd succeed.

"First, we'll do some static movements. Plant your poles like this and raise your right leg, keeping the ski tips up." He spent the next fifteen minutes getting her used to the feel of the equipment before moving on to sliding forward with the use of her poles and then to side-stepping back up the hill.

"Now comes the fun part, falling down and learning how to get back up."

"Do you mean there's a technique to falling in the snow?"

"Of course. There's the safe way and then there's the way you fell the other day. Let me show you."

Before she knew it, Lucky's lunch break was over and she had her lesson with the ski instructor. She worked with Emerald on turning, slowing down, and stopping without falling. By the time they'd made one run down the beginners' slope, the hour was up.

The time had come for her to face the mountain alone.

The beginner's slope may have looked like a gentle hill to someone else, but to her, it was gigantic. After waiting in the lift line, she side-stepped in place to let the lift chair pick her up. So far, so good, she thought when she didn't fall out and managed to lower the safety bar without dropping her poles.

It had been far easier the first day when she hadn't known what could go wrong. No one sat beside her so she had one less thing to worry about when she had to get off. Approaching the top, she opened the safety bar and lifted up the tips of her skis as she crossed the entry ramp. She successfully stood up and slid down the ski ramp and the chair passed beside her. The lift operators had made a snow dragon, complete with sunglasses. Even that didn't knock her off balance.

She dug in the snow with both insteps doing the snowplow to slow to a stop. Her heart raced; the perspiration on her forehead cooled as she stood there. When she looked up, all she could think about was how many bones she could break, which muscles she could pull, and that her grandfather had been right to keep her from it. Of all the wild ideas in her life, facing this fear had to be the hardest.

A skier whizzed by her and she realized that she had to move from the congested exit ramp. She gingerly lightened the pressure from her instep and straightened her skis so she glided down the hill. By the time she managed to stop, she was near the far edge of the slope and couldn't remember how to turn. Sweat broke out on her cold face and a sudden heat wave opened all the pores on her body. Her thermal undergarments were soaked and she was about to cry when she remembered that this was supposed to be fun.

A quick glance around showed her that Lucky wasn't near. Thank goodness for small favors.

She planted her poles and edged her skis around. All of a

sudden, she headed straight down the hill. Keep your balance, she cried to herself. Shift your weight to one side and you'll turn the instructor had said. She turned and slowed down then gained courage and decided against stopping completely. Shifting her weight to the other leg, she turned again. Although she knew she squatted down too much, leaned too far forward and her movements were jerky, she also knew she was skiing! Inching her body upward helped her relax and soon she turned left, then right, then left again. She looked ahead and saw the lift line and realized that the run had come to an end.

As she stood in the lift line, she looked up at the mountain and grinned. The fear was gone; the sense of accomplishment, thrilling. She boldly stepped into place and the lift chair gently hit the back of her knees, signaling her to sit down. She immediately lowered the safety bar and searched the skiers below for Lucky. He wasn't there. She exited with more confidence at the top of the beginners' slope and didn't even try to stop until she was clear of the area.

"A few more runs and you'll be ready for the beginners' portion off the yellow lift," a familiar voice called to her from behind. Just the sound of Lucky's voice boosted her heartbeat.

"I made it down last time without falling," she boasted.

"Good for you. Mind if I join you?"

"Only if you go first and ski slow. That way I can try to imitate you."

"The sincerest form of flattery, I've heard." He made a wide turn, and she dutifully followed.

They stopped above a snow gun for a moment. "How can they make snow when it's this warm? It must be 34 degrees."

"It was freezing when they began, around three this morning. The snowmakers can make it up to around 35 degrees. Sometimes they use the wet snow to pack down into a better base. Gunther, the man over the whole operation, takes pride in the grooming. Groomer Joe White does wonders. Today we have no 'Carolina hardpack,' that's 'ice' to some people. It's a great day to ski."

Lucky led with five turns and stopped on the slope near

where the lift ran overhead. She stopped after three turns and listened as he called up to a man on the lift.

"Close the bar!"

"What?" the skier replied.

"Close the bar," Lucky repeated and even Em knew he meant to lower the safety bar.

After a pause, the skier reached into his jacket, pulled out a silver flask, and dropped it down to the slope below. It took a moment to register, then Em laughed. "Did you say 'Last Call' by mistake?"

Suddenly, her skis slipped out from under her. Before she could react, she slid down the hill, skis and poles in four different directions. Snow flew up partially blinding her view, but she knew she headed directly toward Lucky. His back was to her, and he still stared up at the man on the lift.

"Lucky!" she managed to yell, but didn't have time to get in the warning "watch out." Her skis popped off, stopping quickly, thanks to the brakes built into the bindings. Sliding sideways, her back slammed into his legs and he toppled backward over her.

With his grunt still ringing in her ears, all she could say was "I've found a very inefficient way to stop."

Lucky looked up as he lay on his back in the snow and groaned.

"Are you hurt?" Em asked, heart racing as she realized she could have seriously damaged his legs, or back, or something.

"That'll cost you a dollar," Bob, another ski patroller called down from his lift chair. "Fifty cents each because Jane's in the chair behind me."

Lucky waved up in recognition, then answered Em. "Only my wallet's been damaged. How about you?"

"I'll probably feel it tomorrow but right now nothing's hurt. What did he mean?"

"A little competition among the pro patrollers. Each fall costs fifty cents per witness. Until now, I'd had the lowest record posted on the board."

"Do you mean that groan I almost panicked over was for a dollar?"

"Not just a dollar. It was over losing bragging rights. I hadn't been caught crashing until today. My perfect record's gone." He sat up and brushed the snow off his jacket. "You'll have to make it up to me, you know."

She gulped. "I'll pay the fine."

"Nothing that simple. Have dinner with me."

"I don't know if breaking your record is worth that sacrifice." She pushed his legs off hers. She scrambled out from under him and looked around for her equipment.

He gathered up her skis and poles. "Any night you want, except tomorrow night. I'm meeting your mother at the hospital."

"Why not Saturday night after you get started on my closet?"

"I haven't had time to work up an estimate."

"Skip the estimate. I trust you'll give me a fair price. It's a deal," she added quickly.

"Saturday's fine and I'll give you an estimate then. It's my way of doing business. Come on, let's finish this run and go up again. Only this time, I'll ski behind you."

~

Late that afternoon as soon as she opened her front door, the phone rang. Thinking it was Lucky, she answered with, "Miss me already?"

There was a moment of silence before a woman's voice said, "Maybe I have reached a wrong number. Is this the Graham's residence?"

Momentarily chagrined, she recovered quickly. "Yes. I'm Emerald Graham. May I help you?"

"I was a friend of your grandfather's, otherwise I'd never call a customer like this, you understand?"

"Yes, go on." Em clutched the receiver with both hands.

"I work for the electric company. We've sent three late-payment notices to your accountant but he still hasn't paid. Miss Graham, the electricity at your house will be cut off tomorrow unless you pay up."

"You must be joking!"

"No. Your grandfather helped me with an investment one time and this call is my way of paying him back. Call them tomorrow if you don't believe me."

The disconnecting click registered faster than the message in her brain. What's happened to my estate? She quickly punched in her accountant's number but only reached his answering machine. Tomorrow morning on her way to teaching, she would stop by the electric company and pay this bill.

~

The next evening, Lucky met Lynette at the main entrance of the Watauga County Medical Center. She hugged her purse closely to her chest and her head was lowered but bobbed up every few minutes to see if he'd arrived. He had the idea that had he been late, she would not have stayed.

"Thanks for coming, Lynette. My uncle's been pesterin' me ever since I told him that you have a flower garden. He also volunteers with the Daniel Boone Gardens. He's gonna talk you out of some cuttings from some of your plants."

"I thought I was here to help with the hospital."

Lucky motioned her to step inside to the lounge where his Uncle Harley was to meet them. "That, too," he said as they sat next to each other on the sofa. "Emerald said that you spend hours in the garden when the weather's pretty."

"That's true, but I'm careful to keep protected from the sun."

"Especially up here where the atmosphere's so thin," Lucky added.

"I'm afraid that I won't be able to do this hospital work. Emerald says that women's liberation passed me by and she's right. My only job was to raise Emerald—which was a joy to do. Father Graham took care of everything else after my husband passed away. Emerald said she told you about his accident."

"Yes, she did."

"When her grandfather fell ill last year, she came right home to help me and has stayed by my side ever since. I don't know what I'd do without her. The financial statements might as well have been in a foreign language."

"I think you're smarter than you give yourself credit for. Look at what you accomplished with your flowers. I understand from Em that you designed the layout yourself. You picked flowers that would bloom at different times and studied which fertilizers would work right."

"I did do that, but anyone with time and a little effort could do the same thing."

"There are millions of failed and frustrated gardeners in the world who would argue with that." Lucky realized that she had a hard time accepting a compliment. "When your father-in-law had a stroke, you didn't turn all his care over to someone else. You questioned doctors and medical suppliers and took care of him. Yes siree! You're one competent woman."

Lynette actually blushed. Lucky looked up as his uncle walked off the elevator.

Harley reached for Lynette's hand. "You must be Lynette. Lucky here made me happier than a bear with honey when he said you might volunteer. We'll go on up and see the babies before I give you the grand tour." Harley tucked her hand on his arm as if it were the most natural place for it. "That's a lovely blue sweater you're wearing. Handmade, isn't it?"

Lynette nodded. Harley chatted with her as they wound their way through the hospital.

Lucky tagged along behind them and hid a smile. Harley would have plenty to talk about to Em's mother, and the man could be a charmer to the ladies. Ever since his wife had died a few years back, Harley had helped the hospital in any way he could to repay the kindnesses he'd received when he'd most needed them.

An hour later, Lynette's green eyes were shining in a way that reminded Lucky of Em's eyes. Before, when they'd been lowered, he hadn't noticed them. Lynette stood tall as she looked up at Harley, and Lucky was struck with how beautiful a woman she was. Em would look just like that when she reached her fifties.

"Did I give you a hankerin' to join the volunteers?" Harley asked.

"You make it sound so rewarding. How could I refuse?" Lynette glanced at Lucky before clutching her purse.

They agreed on a schedule and Lucky walked Lynette to her car. "I'm so glad my daughter met you, Lucky. You've been good for both of us." She paused, then added, "I doubt that Emerald would have agreed this morning when she could barely get out of bed."

"Did she tell you about knocking me down on the slope?"

"Yes, but only after praising you for helping her get the most out of her ski lesson, for rescuing her, and for making her feel good. She's always so analytical that normally she can't describe the people she comes in contact with. But she had all the details right about you, even down to the size sweater you wear."

"She did?" Lucky asked, his heart all of a sudden singing. He barely remembered to wish Lynette safe driving as she got into her car and drove away. Maybe the gulf between a wealthy college math professor and a poor jock was really just a small ditch after all.

Chapter 5

"Sorry I didn't have time to empty the closet," Em said on Saturday morning as the two of them entered her grandfather's room. "These boxes are for charity clothes. If someone in your family could use them, feel free to take them."

Lucky stiffened and responded more harshly than he'd intended. "We don't take charity. You donate them to the RAMs Rack, and we'll buy them from there."

She stepped away. "I wasn't implying that you were destitute and needed them. I only wanted to make sure someone got some use out of them. Grandfather always bought the best."

Lucky rubbed his hand across his face and released a pent-up breath. "Sorry, I over-reacted. Grandma always said that we didn't have much but our pride. Sometimes we had more of that than sense if you ask me."

"Pride can carry a person a long way. At times when I wanted to quit college, Grandfather would say, 'A Graham never fails in a responsibility or a task taken on.' I take pride in my family's tradition of success."

"That's not the kind I'm talking about. Grandma has survivor's pride. My grandfather disappeared twenty some odd years ago, but Grandma was sure he didn't leave on his own. She thought he was killed and pestered the sheriff to look all over the county for him. There was talk that he'd hit middle age and wanted a younger wife. Anyone who knew him knew that wasn't true."

"How dreadful for her. He never came back?"

"No. I kind of think she's still waiting for him." Em made it easy to talk about difficult things.

She broke the silence that followed. "What's the RAMs Rack?"

"It's a thrift shop founded by some of the churches in town, the Resort Area Ministries. They also help the volunteer ski patrol programs at the other ski slopes. Sugar Mountain has its own programs."

"I'll check the pockets of Grandfather's suits and box them up while you bring in your tools. This won't take me long."

"Where will you be this morning, in case I have any questions about the closet?"

"Right by your side, I hope. I can hand you tools and things while you work."

Her wide open eyes fairly shimmered with eagerness. He'd hate to disappoint her. "This isn't very exciting. You sure you want to help?"

"It's all new to me. I've never had to fix anything, hammer a nail or tighten a screw. It's about time I learned, don't you think?"

"I know better than to refuse an offer of help. If you'll hold the end of the tape measure in that corner, we'll take better measurements than we took the other day."

Lucky did his best not to bump into Em while they worked, but it couldn't be helped. After he drilled a hole, he backed up against her. She wanted to use the screw gun so he had to hold her hands in the correct position. As he had his arms around her and his fingers on top of hers, she leaned into him. Her hair played across his chin. If he didn't move soon, work would be forgotten. "Do you have a good grip?" At her nod, he released her hands and stepped away.

The questions she asked reminded him of his ten-year-old nephew. "Why don't you do it this way? Am I holding this right? Do you measure to the edge or the middle of that hole?" One question on top of the other.

"Aren't all screws the same?"

"Not in my experience," he said, his expression deadpan.

She giggled and swatted his arm. "Naughty man. There's so much to learn. Why don't they at least make all screw heads either straight or crossed, one or the other?"

"Em, one more question and I'll lock you out of the room."

"You wouldn't dare," she teased but lost her smile when he started toward her. "Oh, no you don't," she said backing up. "I'll be quiet. I won't say another word."

He stopped and looked at her. "Impossible."

She shook her head and pointed to the job to be done and they went back to work in the deepest corner of the closet.

Exactly two minutes later—he checked his watch—she blurted, "What about lunch? I'm famished. Aren't we at a good stopping point?"

"I warned you," he said and reached for her arm to lead her out of the room.

"We'll see about that," she taunted. She squatted down on the floor to evade him. She grabbed the carpet to anchor herself. It pulled loose instead. "Now what have I done?"

"Let me see." Lucky peeled back the carpet to check the tack strips. "What's this?" He removed a large manila envelope hidden underneath.

"Too thin to be love letters," Em said, shaking the envelope.

"Too well hidden to be stock certificates," added Lucky.

"Too flat to be the skeleton you asked me about earlier."

"And too light to be emeralds," Lucky said. "Are you going to open it?"

"What if it's bad news or something that could change my life? I might be better off to put it back."

"Now you've seen it, would you be able to forget about it?"

"You're right," she said and ripped open one end. Inside was a single sheet of paper. "A map?"

"A treasure map!" he yiped. "Oooh."

"Impossible. Why would Grandfather have a treasure map? Why hide it? Why not search for the loot himself?"

"Maybe he hid something he didn't want found in his lifetime."

"That's possible, I suppose." She peered closely at the map. "The notes are in his handwriting."

A search of the envelope revealed no other papers. "Let's get out of this closet and into better light. He left this to be found. Otherwise, it would have been destroyed."

Lucky lowered the hospital bed and they sat side by side, thighs touching as they bent over the map. "This is in Mitchell County. It's less than an hour from here."

"That close? It would have been easy for Grandfather to go there."

"Maybe this was an extra copy he kept hidden. He could have taken the treasure long ago."

She shook her head. "I inherited his penchant for details. He wouldn't have forgotten something like this." She hesitated, then looked at him. "We both know it can't be a treasure, but it's fun to think so."

Her eyes were such a clear green that Lucky automatically nodded. It was a moment before his thoughts became coherent. "Could someone else have hidden it in the closet?"

"That's not likely. The guest bedrooms are on the first floor and visitors don't generally come upstairs. That leaves Mother, our housekeeper and me."

Lucky studied the map. "I think this 'X' is very near some acres my grandpa put in my name when I was born. It's remote. I'm not sure the road's passable anymore."

"Haven't you visited the property lately?"

"It's been five or six years. Grandpa had specific written instructions attached to the deed. Those two hundred acres could never be developed and the timber could not be sold off. Parts of it are so steep that I've been happy to let nature be the only developer. There's even a small pocket of virgin timber near some cliffs."

She took the map from his hands and twisted around to lie on her stomach on the hard bed.

Lucky hesitated and then lay beside her, his chin propped up on his fists. "The 'X' is in a steep area. Look at all those topography lines running close together. Each one's a hundred feet. Was your grandfather in good physical shape?"

"He was a little overweight, but he liked to hunt, I think. At least he had a collection of guns." She paused, then added, "This note says to watch for fallen rocks at the bend."

"Hum." Lucky turned his head to look at her rather than the map.

"Are you thinking what I'm thinking?"

"No way. You need to wait until spring," Lucky said, bolting upright.

"You have a four-wheel-drive truck and you know the area," she coaxed, twisting to sit up beside him.

"It's winter, and I doubt I could even find that dirt road much less drive very far on it," he countered, then made the mistake of looking into her eyes.

"The sun's shining and at that lower altitude, the snow's probably already melted."

He swallowed. "We won't be able to do much more than locate the general area," he said with obvious reluctance. "We'd need to find the land owner to get permission to trespass."

"I hadn't thought of that."

"We'd have to start out early one morning to hike in and do some exploring."

"Does this mean we're in this together?" she asked.

"I guess it does." His immediate reward was a smile.

"Let's go right after lunch today and stake out the area. We could go back tomorrow for the whole day."

"Not tomorrow. But we can plan it for another Saturday, weather permitting." At her momentary deflation, he added, "Sunday lunch at Grandma's is a tradition I'm not about to change. Since we're taking off this afternoon, I'll have to come over tomorrow to finish up this closet and do the next one on the list."

"I don't mind the delay."

"I do. I have a contract and I *will* meet the deadlines as stated. I have a reputation to uphold."

"Pride in a job well done. We'll do it your way." She jumped off the bed. "What are we waiting for? Let's eat and be on our way."

"Wear hiking boots and warm clothes that you won't mind getting dirty. There's no telling what kind of terrain we'll run into."

As they sat down to lunch, the phone rang. Em answered it in the hall, and Lucky watched a frown crease her forehead. He couldn't hear the conversation.

"Sorry about the interruption," Em said, returning to the table. "I just found out that my accountant is out of town this week."

After lunch, he asked to borrow an old towel. He opened the creaking passenger door of his truck, revealing a ripped seat crudely repaired with strips of duct tape. He laid the towel over the seat. "Hambone usually sits there and it's easier to cover it up than to get out all the dog hairs." He moved a box of tools from the floorboard to the back before he let her get in.

"We'll take Highway 105 down the mountain, then pick up 221. You buckled in? Ready?" He started the Explorer.

"Aye, aye, Captain. The weather's holdin' and it looks like clear sailing."

Lucky laughed. "It be pirate treasure we're lookin' for then?"

"Naturally. We're looking for stolen loot, plundered from poor trusting folks. Pirates killed and robbed the rich and poor alike and kept the jewels and gold, not like Robin Hood."

"Then it's blood money buried in the ground. I'm not sure I like the sound of that," he said, pretending to shiver.

"You're right. We'll make it the pot of gold at the end of the rainbow."

"Keep in mind that your grandfather probably buried it. Maybe he was a spy, or witnessed a murder, but he didn't want to get involved. We might be looking for old papers or newspaper clippings he wanted to keep quiet until after his death."

"That's a sobering thought. Enough of this speculation; we'll find out on the next trip."

On the farside of Foscoe, Em pointed to the ice-covered cliffs beside the road. "They look like curtains and curtains of icicles draped over each other."

"They look good now, but once the temperatures warms, all that clear ice turns milky white, refreezing."

"Oh look, Grandfather Mountain's cliffs are covered with ice, too. See how they gleam in the sun? From this angle, you can tell where the mountain got its name."

"The old man's snoozing away." Lucky eased off on the gas. "The turnoff to Sugar Mountain's coming up soon. I'll bet the slopes are crowded today. Weekends are busy days. There are usually plenty of volunteer patrollers to help out, though."

"How did you get started skiing?"

"I was raised near Banner Elk. Lots of my cousins worked winters at the slopes. I started out working in ski rentals at night after school and weekends in seventh grade."

"Did you have to go to work so young?" she asked.

He nodded. "Dad died when I was ten, and my grandfather disappeared before that. My uncles and aunts helped Grandma all they could, but it was still kinda rough on all of us. Mostly we grew our own vegetables, butchered our own meat, and gathered roots in season to sell for school clothes and supplies. This area used to be real tough on families who weren't self-sufficient."

"But you survived."

"We did more than that. The whole family worked together, played together, went to church on Sundays."

"What came next for you at Sugar?"

"I worked a year when I turned eighteen as a lift operator and the next year as a snow-maker. I skied every chance I got. After high school, I took night and weekend classes for emergency medical training. I've been a ski patroller for ten years now."

"You're good at it. You seem to love it."

"Yeah, I do. What about you? How did a pretty woman

like you get so interested in math?"

"Some people would interpret that as a sexist remark, but I'll let it pass." Em took a deep breath and thought about her childhood, trying not to bring back the loneliness she had grown up with. "I've always liked numbers and math comes easily to me. My father taught me to play chess before I was in first grade. Those are the fondest memories I have of him," she said with a sigh. "And the last. On rainy days, we'd have marathon sessions and Mother would personally serve our lunch in the library so we wouldn't have to stop playing. Looking back, I think she encouraged the matches because it gave us something to do together."

"I hear there are chess tournaments for children."

"We didn't know about them then." Thank goodness, she silently added since a big part of her fascination with the game was to play with her father.

"Did you do anything special with your mother?"

"She would brush my long hair, for hours it seemed." Em smiled at Lucky before continuing. "Sometimes she'd play Barbie with me; sometimes we'd read stories aloud. We spent a lot of time together, partly because Father was out of town a lot."

Lucky's inquiring glance prompted her to explain. "Mother thought it was due to work. We later found out he had a passion for extreme skiing. He'd spend weeks at a time in the winter in Austria or Alaska. In the summer, he went to South America."

"Living every skier's dream. I take it your mother didn't ski."

"She was too timid to try and too shy of the crowds. I talked her into going to therapy once, but Grandfather ridiculed her so that ended that."

"There's no one stopping her now."

Em shook off the dark cloud in her mind. Her grandfather accomplished much in the community, stock brokers admired him, and he provided well for his family. That he wanted to be utter ruler of all he surveyed had seemed a small price for his family to pay. She sat up straighter.

"That's a good idea. Not that I mind her depending on me so much, you understand, because it's my way of returning the love she showered on me when I was growing up. But I think she'd be happier if she were more outgoing. She wants to be, but she loses her nerve easily."

"You went to Watauga High School," Lucky said, remembering that calculus class so long ago.

"At first, but I transferred for my last two years to a boarding school in Virginia. It was known for its math program. I missed being home, but I had some great teachers. Then I went to college in Canada and graduate school at Vanderbilt. That's my whole history."

"You left out the good parts. What about the guy who got you interested in karate?"

"He was exciting. But he wanted to spend ten years traveling the globe." With my money, she added silently. "I wasn't interested in doing that—I'm too much of a homebody at heart."

"And the swimmer?"

"He went to California for graduate work, and we drifted apart. It was fun while it lasted. What about you? What happened to the women in your life?"

"Nothing serious. I've never lived with anyone, never been tempted. In some ways, I suppose I'm out of step with the times. I believe in love and the kind of marriage that lasts a lifetime. Until that comes along, I'm content to date, although I hate that word."

"So do I. It sounds so—'fifties'." She stared at his profile for a moment, amazed at herself. Em looked out the window. Two mountains ahead had their sides chiseled to sheer rock walls by mining machines.

Lucky slowed the truck. "Feldspar came out of some of the early Spruce Pine mines."

"Weren't there also some emerald mines near here?"

"Sure enough. I forgot you're an emerald hound. Emeralds were found by two men in the late 1800s on Crabtree Mountain. That's where we're headed. My land's on part of that mountain."

"Are you serious? We'll be on the *very* mountain that at least one of my specimens came from." Her voice quivered with excitement. She sat forward in the seat. "How much further?"

"We head three miles southwest of town. I thought we could start there."

They swung off Highway 19 onto a narrow paved road, Lucky eased the Explorer onto a private dirt road. He shifted into four wheel drive and churned on for half a mile before stopping by a downed tree. "We're on foot from here. Next time I'll bring a chain saw."

Em shivered as she stepped from the warm truck onto the crunchy dirt beside the road.

"Hoarfrost," he said.

"Whore frost?" she repeated. "Why?"

He laughed. "That ice that pushes its way up from the ground and softens the dirt. It crunches when you step on it." He walked toward her to demonstrate. "Some call the stuff on the tree limbs 'fog frost'." He pulled out a compass then looked around. "Let's walk the road for a mile then cut off to the right. Here's a roll of orange surveyor tape for you. Mark the trail, especially at the turns."

She dropped the tape into her pocket then zipped up her down jacket. She scrambled over the tree blocking the road. "When do we get to your property?"

"We're on it. That's why the road's not maintained. It keeps trespassers out. Damn. Deer hunters. See the shell casings?"

She stopped short. "We won't be shot by accident, will we?"

"Deer season's in the fall. Nothing's in season now—not that that'll stop some folks. Critters have it hard enough just surviving the winter."

"Do you hunt?" she asked as they continued their walk.

He nodded. "I usually get a deer for me and another one for Grandma, to last us over the winter. Nothing's quite as good as smoked deer sausage on pizza." He saw her stricken expression. "You have to remember that my dad raised cattle for hard cash. Culling out a buck deer to help my family is an important part of my life. One buck's equivalent to a steer, fifty chickens or two good-sized hogs. It's a trade-off. Man evolved as meat-eaters and our digestive system's set up for it."

"I know all that. It's just that I've never seen anything killed, except bugs. I'm used to the neat, tidy packages from the grocery store. I hope you don't waste any of it—or make trophies out of the heads."

"Did your grandfather bring home trophies?"

"When he hunted? No, but I don't remember him bringing home any meat either." Em mused. "Maybe it was the one thing he wasn't particularly good at."

"I don't hunt or fish for sport. All life's too precious for that."

"Thank goodness." She hadn't been exposed to this perspective before. She liked it, she realized, and walked with a tiny bounce in her step.

"Why don't you wrap two pieces of surveyor's tape on that branch. Leave long tails so we can spot them on our way back. I'll take another look at this map."

They had walked in silence for several minutes when Lucky turned onto a narrow trail. Em marked a tree with the orange tape.

"We should come to a creek soon, and we'll use it to guide us up the mountain. We'll have to limit ourselves to an hour. Daylight disappears early back in these steep mountains."

"I didn't think about that." Em took a deep breath and looked around. "These woods are beautiful, even in winter. Look at this thick vine running up the tree trunk over there. It's hairy!"

"Don't touch it! Poison ivy keeps its poison all year around. The oil's potent for years after you cut it. You can't even burn it to destroy it because the oil can go airborne."

"I had no idea it could get that big—it's as thick as my fist."

"Poison ivy and kudzu thrive anywhere in the South," Lucky grumbled. "I don't know about poison ivy but hogs are the only way I know of to get rid of kudzu. They dig down and eat the roots of the vine."

"I don't see any kudzu here."

"It's not like the ivy, it disappears with the first hard frost. I read that chemists are trying to come up with a medicinal use for it. Homeowners all over the South will celebrate when they do that."

They walked on a little longer when Lucky stopped. "I reckon the map starts here. If I'm not mistaken, our treasure *is* on my land." He turned from the view to look at Em. "What could your grandfather have had to do with my grandpa's land?"

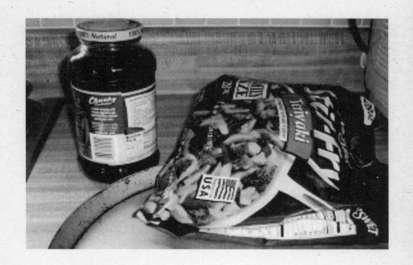

Chapter 6

A shiver ran down Em's spine. "Only one way to find out."

"Not today. As Alice said when she went through the looking glass, this keeps getting curiouser and curiouser."

Doing an about-face, they followed their orange tape markings back to the truck and drove toward Sugar Mountain. "I have all the fixings for a pizza at my house. I'd planned to take you out to dinner, but it'll be too late to change and then go out."

"Pizza? I haven't had that in years. Do we need to stop for any ingredients?"

"It depends. What foods don't you like?"

"Canned peas, brussels sprouts and raw onion."

Lucky chuckled. "We'll have no problem there. 'Course, now my grandma fixes brussels sprouts like no one can resist." Lucky turned off Highway 105 at the stop light and drove past the castle-shaped houses at Tynecastle, past the time-share resort, and turned left into a side entrance to Sugar Mountain Estates.

"You didn't tell me you lived near the ski slope."

"You didn't ask." At first the winding road was crowded with modern chalets, then the houses were built further apart as they climbed. As they passed Sugartop, Lucky muttered, "Those condos are so ugly they got everyone mad enough to pass a ridge law. Now, people can't build on the ridge tops."

Em nodded and Lucky realized that she might know people who owned the property, maybe even the developer.

About a twisting half mile of gravel road further, the road ended at his house. Lucky slowed to give Em time to look.

Em gave a start of surprise. "Oh, my."

The long-sloping dark gray roof covered a deep red, wood-sided first floor trimmed in forest green. At one end of the deck, graceful arcs, borrowed from the home's eyebrow dormer and arched gable windows, took the form of a bow-front pavilion. Below the deck, fieldstone skirting anchored the home solidly in the forest floor.

Lucky parked the Explorer in the driveway. His business occupied the garage. He got out of the truck, opened her door and helped her out, all the while watching her face.

"You knew, didn't you?" she whispered, clinching his hand as recognition awakened long ago dreams.

"It sounded awfully close."

"This is better than my pretend house. It's almost the same as I created with my Barbie dolls. Amazing." She stared at Lucky. How could two people from such different backgrounds dream of the same home?

"Come on in. We'll take the grand tour. Remember, I wasn't expecting visitors." Just then, Lucky heard four huge paws galloping toward them from the woods beside the house. "Get ready to meet Hambone," he warned with only seconds to spare.

"I haven't been around dogs much," she said faintly.

"You had a deprived childhood. Don't worry, Hambone's like a person. He'll be polite since you're with me."

Hambone's head reached Lucky's waist.

"Sit," Lucky said.

Hambone did so.

"Let him smell your hand, then you can pet him."

After the warm nose grazed the back of her hand, Hambone opened his mouth and panted.

"Is he going to bite me?" Em asked, drawing back.

"No, you're too sweet for his liking. He only bites the bad guys. He's giving you approval to pet him."

Em touched gingerly then let her fingers dig into the fur. "His fur's so soft and smooth," she said with a touch of awe. "And warm." Hambone leaned into her hands, teaching her all the good spots to massage.

"He probably left Grandma's place as soon as he heard my truck. She lives a quarter of a mile over the hill," he said, jerking his thumb over his shoulder indicating a direction away from the ski slope.

"Does she live in Sugar's resort?" Maybe his family wasn't as poor as he'd led her to believe.

"Heavens no, although a developer would love to buy the place. She refuses to move in case Grandpa comes back in person or so his spirit will know where to find her. He built the cabin and it suits her fine."

"I can't even imagine a love that strong."

"I can." He started up the steps. "Hambone's expecting his supper. I'll feed him first and then get started on ours." She followed him up and onto a wide straight section of the deck with Hambone walking beside her. Lucky opened a glass-paneled door for direct entry into the breakfast nook and to one end of the white kitchen.

Hambone's water dish was as big as a punch bowl and his food container could have held enough chili for eight people.

"What can I do to help?" she asked, feeling a bit lost in a kitchen.

"I didn't think you could cook, with a housekeeper and all."

"I can't do much more than breakfast, but I do know how to set the table." She looked around the large kitchen. "I expected a cabin with a tiny kitchen."

"When I drew up the plans for the house, I decided to build one that I could live in for the rest of my life. I wanted room for children and dogs. My sisters insisted on a big kitchen with a place to eat in it."

"Which contractor did you use?"

"I did most of the work myself but sub-contracted out the plumbing and electrical work."

Her opinion of him raised another notch. "You are a multi-talented guy."

"Let me tell you, it was a challenge. A learn-as-you-do experience. I didn't dig the foundation like Grandpa did, but I did more than I probably should have."

"What do you mean?"

He laughed a short, self-depreciating laugh. "I had to tear out one section of wall because I forgot about a door I'd put in the plan. When the building inspector came, he failed me the first time because I didn't have the right sheet rock for the garage."

"Not many people would take on a project like this. Most people couldn't, much less wouldn't do it."

Lucky took a can of dough out of the refrigerator and started stretching it into a round shape for the pizza pan. "I lived with Grandma for the first six months until I finished the framing and roofing. She's been good to me all my life."

"I envy you having lots of relatives. We're not close to my mom's side of the family. They live in Atlanta. For all practical purposes, it's only my mother and me." Em watched his hands massaging the dough. "I didn't know you could buy dough already made."

"You figure out all kinds of tricks when you live alone. Would you reach in the cabinet over there and get the spaghetti sauce bottle? The deer sausage is in the refrigerator. Then pull any combination of frozen vegetables you like out of the freezer and spread them on a paper towel to thaw."

"Aren't you going to chop up fresh ones?"

"Frozen's a lot easier and keeps me from having to go to the grocery store so often." After he'd worked the dough for a few minutes, Em continued to stare at his hands. "What?" he asked.

"I'm waiting for you to fling it in the air to stretch it."

"Not a chance. Here, you try it."

"Not if you want it to end up in the pan and not the floor."

Lucky showed Em how to put the pizza together and let her top the sauce with mozzarella. He scattered the veggies, meat and spices thickly across the top. As it baked, Lucky took her on a tour of his home. "Excuse the lack of furniture," he said.

"I thought you were trying for a Japanese look—simple and uncluttered."

"I wish. I'm what you could call house-poor. The mortgage claims most of my money. The bed, dresser, and living room sofa were donated from relatives' attics. The TV and disc player I bought. The rest of the furniture will have to wait—at least until we find the treasure."

Does it always come down to money? she asked herself. He lost some points for that one. Just once, she'd like to believe that wealth wasn't part of her attraction.

As they turned the corner from the kitchen to the back of the house, Em stopped and stared down the wide hallway. One side was covered with floor-to-ceiling bookshelves, crammed full of books. Paperbacks, old hardcovers and tattered books with no dust jackets were mixed together with even a few stacks on the floor.

"One day I'll be able to afford new books. In the meantime, I haunt yard sales and the library cast-off section."

"'When I have money, I buy books. If there's any left I buy food'—it's a quote I remember from philosophy class, but I can't remember who said it."

"I can't claim that dedication." Lucky laughed. "But I can admire it." He tugged her away from the stacks and into the living room. He showed Em how to build a fire in the stone fireplace on one side of the open living and dining area.

She sat beside him on the wide sofa and looked at pictures of the house taken at different stages of construction. Doc Watson's music played softly in the background as they shared a couple of beers and ate the pizza. Hambone sprawled out, belly up on the rug in front of the fire.

At last, Em leaned back contentedly. She couldn't remember the last time life was so precious. "Thank you for the unique pizza, for chauffeuring me today, for introducing me to Hambone, and for sharing your home with me."

"Is that an exit speech?"

"Not at all. I wanted to say it when it occurred to me."

He leaned back also, then slid his hand over hers. She squeezed his fingers and let her hand rest in his as she stared into the fire.

"Would you like another beer?" he asked. When she shook her head, he placed both empty glasses on the glass-topped coffee table. Its base was made from a gnarled tree he'd cut down to put up the house. When he rested his arm on the sofa back, she slid closer so her shoulder nestled under his and her face lay against his chest. It felt natural for her to go to him.

She tilted her head up to look at him at the same time he looked down at her. She smiled a secret smile, one tinged with knowledge and excitement, of expectation and hope. His lips brushed hers and he whispered, "You feel good in my arms."

A flush of belonging enveloped her. Had she truly ever been at home anywhere in the world? Her grandfather's house, now her mother's, was always too big and formal. The other places she'd lived were borrowed and temporary. Lucky's home welcomed her from the moment they'd driven up and Hambone had accepted her.

His lips again met hers. This time she parted hers inviting him to stay a little longer, not just to rest but to explore. Beneath her hand resting on his chest, she felt the strong, steady beat of his heart quicken. Her own responded in kind when the tip of his tongue slid between her lips and she tasted the malt flavor of the beer. She strained to get closer and shifted, breaking the kiss.

Nuzzling his neck, she kissed the space between his adam's apple and his chin and finally returned her lips to his. His personal scent washed over her. She needed to get closer.

Suddenly, three shrill ringing tones blared, followed by a woman's voice: "Attention Banner Elk First Responders!"

Chapter 7

Lucky jerked his head up and shushed Em before she could say anything.

"Car observed going off bank on Sugar Top Drive, a quarter mile before the condos."

Without so much as an "excuse me," Lucky jumped off the couch and retrieved his radio from its recharger. "Ten-four. Unit 27 on the way."

Em's overheated body cooled rapidly, leaving her mind slow to catch up. His eyes held both passion and frustration, taking the sting out of the abrupt interruption. He stuffed his shirt tail back into his pants. "I'm sorry about that. Do you want to come along?"

Still reeling from his kisses, she hesitated then said, "If I won't be in the way."

"You might get put to work. Hambone, come on." He grabbed their coats and they strode out to the Explorer.

"Why do you do this?" she asked as Lucky turned onto Sugar Top Drive.

"Because I can. I'm already trained from years on the ski patrol."

"If you went back to school, you could be a nurse or even a doctor and you could do this full time and get paid for it."

"Nah. Then it would be a job. I already have a business, and I like what I do."

"You'll never get rich that way."

"Who said I wanted to be rich?"

"Doesn't everyone in America?" she asked softly, afraid to believe the implications of his question.

"Don't get me wrong. I'd like to make more money. But extreme wealth doesn't motivate me. It doesn't buy what really counts in life." He reached down and briefly squeezed her hand as it rested on the seat between them.

Had she offended him again? Her casual acceptance of wealth as one of the most important elements in her life suddenly made her uneasy.

Within minutes Lucky reduced speed and handed her a high-powered spotlight to plug into the cigarette lighter.

"I'll drive along the shoulder and you tell me what you see over the bank. Look for broken shrubs, matted grass, skinned trees. Anything that would indicate that a car went over the bank."

"I don't see anything yet," Em said, balancing the top part of her body out the passenger window to get a better view as he drove slowly. The cold air stimulated her face, but the wind made her squint. "Nothing yet," she repeated. "Are you sure we're at the right place?" she asked a few minutes later.

"It's the worst turn on this part of the road. I'm going to drive around and try again."

Frustration was evident in his voice. They repeated the quarter mile search and Lucky was ready to turn around again when Em cried out, "There! I think I saw something shiny."

Lucky parked the Explorer well on the shoulder and stood

outside her window. He shone the spotlight in the direction she pointed. "Hello," he shouted. The car was overturned two hundred feet down the embankment, wedged between two trees. "I'm Lucky with the First Responders. Is anyone hurt?" He waited for a reply, then called again. Still no reply.

Lucky reached for his radio and called in the location and finished with "requesting an ambulance and rescue truck." He gave Em an extra flashlight to shine down the embankment for him and set out road flares to highlight the location.

"Hambone," he called, then kneeled down to take the dog's head in his hands and look him in the eyes. "Go find the people. Let me know where they are."

Hambone barked once and headed down the steep incline.

Lucky turned to Em. "You ever use a two-way radio?"

She shook her head.

"Here, push this to talk. Stay with the truck so you can send other First Responders down to me."

She stepped out of the truck as he looped rope through the bottom of the first aid pack and loaded it onto his shoulders.

"Be careful," she said.

In a surprise move, he kissed her hard on the mouth. "This isn't exactly how I wanted the evening to go."

"Wild things happen when you're around." She'd never felt so alive.

"I hope it won't run you off."

"Not on your life, buddy. Go." She gave him a gentle push and down the hill he went, leaping and sliding. A car drove up with another close behind.

"Lucky got here first, didn't he?" a woman called, slamming the door of the first car.

"You don't sound surprised," Em said to the compact woman striding up beside her.

She laughed. "He's quick and knows his medicine. He answers all the calls, even one like this where you have an idea that it's just some drunk who took the curve at eighty mile-an-hour. And Hambone's always with him, doing exactly what Lucky asks him to."

"You sound like you know him well."

"I'm Maggie. Lucky's my cousin. Our kin's scattered all over these mountains. You never know if one of these calls is for someone you know. I suspect that's part of the reason he answers them so fast."

They heard the crash of breaking glass from down the bank and the muted voices of the three men now working the accident. "What was that?" Em cried, more concerned for Lucky than the accident victim.

Before she could raise the radio to her lips, Maggie said, "I'm not sure. We have to wait it out. Our questions would only distract them. But it sure is hard to stand here and wait."

Of course she was right, but Em's finger twitched on the call button. It was irritating not to have an instant answer.

"Em," Lucky's voice squawked over the radio, "when the ambulance gets here, we'll need a backboard tied to a rope to haul him out of here."

She pushed the button on the radio and yelled into the speaker, "Okay. I'll tell them."

Maggie cleared her throat. "You can release the button now. Next time, all you have to say is 'ten-four.' And don't raise your voice—all he'll hear is static."

Dismay at her poor performance stilled Em's tongue. The ambulance arrived and Maggie nudged Em to relay Lucky's message.

"Don't worry, Honey. You did fine. We'll make a rescuer out of you yet," Maggie said as the ambulance crew lowered the equipment over the side.

Em's job was done. She spared a moment to look over her companion, the first responder who identified herself as Lucky's cousin. Maggie hadn't inherited Lucky's height or his Roman nose, though she shared his athleticism Em noted as she skidded down the hill and helped deliver the backboard to the accident. Em felt awkward just standing and not doing anything. She hoped the person wasn't hurt too bad; hoped they were able to help fast enough.

The man and dog on her mind scrambled up over the embankment at that moment. "You're bleeding!" Em's heart pounded when she saw the light pick up blood on Lucky's face.

"Huh? I'm not hurt. I ran into some brambles on the way down." Even though he panted from his quick climb up the bank, he stood a moment to grasp her by the back of the neck and plant a kiss on her lips—in front of his cousin.

"What was that for?" Em asked, pleased but embarrassed.

"For being here, for sharing this with me. I'll only be a few more minutes," Lucky said.

"I'm not going anywhere," she murmured to his back as he strode past her to speak with an ambulance attendant. She remembered the First Responder beside her. "I'm Em Graham," she said. "Nice to meet you."

"Are you related to the Boone Grahams or the Tater Hill Grahams?"

Em cleared her throat, startled by the question. "Umm—Boone."

"Lucky sure is lucky sometimes," she said. She smiled at her own pun and left when Lucky came back.

"How injured was the driver?" Em asked Lucky later as they drove back.

"He had a dislocated shoulder. Both car doors were jammed between the trees and we had to take him out through the rear glass. No seat belt, drunk as a Tequila worm, didn't feel a thing. Every muscle in his body will be screaming at him tomorrow."

"Maybe next time he'll think before drinking too much."

"Maybe," Lucky said, clasping her hand. "Where to? The choice is yours—my place or yours?" He was obviously still pumped up on adrenalin from the rescue.

His smile took her back to a few hours ago in front of the fire. She looked at the clock on the dash. One-twenty in the morning. She sighed, energy draining from her despite her best efforts. He may be used to this kind of excitement, but she wasn't. "It's late. I'm afraid it'll have to be my place. We've had a full day."

"That we have. Old Hambone back there is all tuckered out."

"We put a lot of miles on this truck today. At least let me

pay for the gas since the Spruce Pine trip was my idea."

"I thought we were partners in that deal. It's on my land."

A smile tugged at the corners of her mouth. "Sixty-forty sounds reasonable to me."

"Seventy-five, twenty-five. Possession rules the day around here. If your tree falls on my land, the tree is mine to cut up."

"Fifty-fifty and not a point lower," she insisted.

"Agreed. You drive a hard bargain."

"Thank you, kind sir. I learned it at my grandfather's knee. Speaking of him, would you like to go to a dinner with me in his honor? I was told I could bring a guest."

"It depends on what's involved."

She heard the caution in his voice. "Suit and tie at the Elk Creek Inn at seven this Wednesday night."

He groaned. "Are you sure you want to take a poor country boy like me to a wing-ding? I wouldn't know how to act."

"Don't act, be yourself. You'll love the food. Sometimes they have farm-raised alligator, pheasant, and venison, all flown in from licensed sellers."

"Now I've heard everything. Venison's considered exotic?"

"You know what I mean." She looked at his profile outlined by the oncoming vehicle headlights. "Please say 'yes.' I'd rather have someone there I know besides Mother."

"Do I get to escort two beautiful ladies?"

"Unless Mother comes up with her first date in twenty years, yes."

"I'll pick you up at six thirty. Who and why honor your grandfather? He's been gone for a year."

"Just before his stroke, he gave money for a building for the geology department. He stipulated that the Stock Club pay for the equipment and computers."

"The 'Stock Club'? Was he a cattleman?"

Em swallowed a laugh. "Stocks like the stock market. He bought shares in businesses. When people started asking his advice, he became a broker and wrote a column for different newspapers. He had an excellent record and helped loads of people get rich. Some of those people will be there Wednesday."

"I don't know anything about stocks."

"You don't have to. You can sit between Mother and me and charm us so that we won't have to worry about talking with anyone else. Grandfather knew these people, but we didn't have much contact with them. It's an obligation, as well as an honor for our family, but you'll save us from the boredom."

"I'll do my best," Lucky said as he drove into her driveway and killed the engine. He reached over and brushed her bangs away from her eyes then rested his hand on her neck. She leaned toward him.

"What time will you be here tomorrow?" she asked, her lips close to his.

"One o'clock. I plan to do your bedroom next, so you may want to empty out the closet while I finish your grandfather's."

Her kiss was gentle and wistful, and then she went into the house without looking back.

Chapter 8

Late Sunday morning Em made the tenth trip from her walk-in closet to lay clothes on the bed, chairs and floor while her mother told her about her first day volunteering at the hospital.

"Harley was right. Sitting and holding those preemies felt wonderful. I rocked and rocked and found myself humming."

"Did you do that for me when I was a baby?"

"Of course I did. I even hummed to you before you were born. Don't you remember?" she teased.

"I vaguely remember feeling a rumble. I thought it was hunger pains."

Lynette laughed a light, silvery laugh, and Em involuntarily stared at her. Her mother's face had lost its pallor and her cheeks glowed.

"I haven't heard you laugh in a long time," Em said. "I've missed it."

Lynette's smile faded but didn't disappear. "It's been too long, dear. I've cooped myself up in this big old house and hidden from the world. I—I've wanted to change but I didn't have the courage until Lucky practically forced me. He gave me the push I needed to get back into life."

"You've been hiding here since Dad died, haven't you?"

Lynette released a deep breath. "Has it been nearly twenty-five years?"

Em sat beside her mother in a small space between stacks of clothes on the bed and took her hand, gladdened at how freely her mother spoke to her, almost as if she were a peer instead of a daughter. "I've never asked before, but did Grandfather have anything to do with your marrying Dad?"

Lynette blanched but answered in a gentle voice. "My father and your grandfather were friends. They made Byron an offer to marry me that was so sweet that he couldn't refuse." At Em's raised eyebrow, Lynette continued. "Father was such a forceful man that I was intimidated by him all my life. He had absolute dictatorial power over me, and I didn't dare question it. The whole women's liberation of the 70s and 80s passed me by. I didn't have the power to challenge anything he planned for me."

Squeezing Em's hand, she rose and paced. "One afternoon Father introduced me to the man I was to marry in two months. That man was Byron."

Em gasped.

"I've never told you this before because I was so ashamed of myself for being relieved. Relieved that I wouldn't have to date or worry about catching a husband, as it was called in those days. Byron was attractive and always treated me with the utmost respect. I would only have changed one thing."

"What was that?"

"We wanted more children; I would have loved a house full. We thought we had more time. I came to love your father very much."

"I remember you smiling up at him whenever he was home, which wasn't often."

"The arrangement included an apartment in New York where Byron stayed two weeks out of the month to keep up with the stock market."

Emeralds in the Snow

"I didn't know you'd been to New York."

"I haven't. Byron invited me but I didn't dare go. It was too busy for me, too many people rushing by on the sidewalks. I would have been miserable and that would have made Byron unhappy. I have no desire to visit a city. Seeing movies of them is enough for me. I'm not like you."

"I've spent enough time in the city. Boone suits me fine."

"I meant that you're not afraid to try things. People don't frighten you. Why, you stood up to your grandfather as soon as you could talk and walk at the same time."

"I didn't win very many arguments."

"But you tried. That's the point, I never even tried." Lynette squarely faced Em who still sat on the bed. "I'm trying from now on. I gathered all my courage to meet Lucky at the hospital that day and nothing bad happened to me. On the contrary, good experiences have happened ever since."

"Like what?" Em said, tuning in to her mother's excitement.

The doorbell rang, interrupting them. "I'll tell you about all that later."

"Hi," Lucky said softly, absorbing the impact of seeing her again. The alabaster skin on her face was flawless in the bright January sun streaming over his shoulder. She'd been the last thought in his mind the night before and the first image in his head this morning. "Am I too early?"

"No, come on in. Mother was helping me clear the closet. We're almost finished."

He followed her upstairs and into her bedroom, an intimate act under other circumstances. But her bed was already full— of clothes.

"I heard good things about you," he said to Lynette as she dropped another load of clothes on the bed.

"You did?" she said with a lilt in her voice.

"I heard that you looked like an angel holding those babies and they cooed and smiled when you talked to them." Lucky watched the blush creep up her neck and flush her cheeks. "I also heard that you asked my uncle out for a date."

Em sputtered. "What's this?"

"A double date, to be precise," Lynette said primly, then frowned. "Was I too forward?"

"No! Not at all. Where? When?" Em asked.

"Since I agreed to go with you to the dinner in honor of your grandfather, the next logical step was to ask someone along for me," Lynette said with confidence. Quickly she reverted to her shy self and added, "Is that all right with you? Was I wrong?"

Em laughed and hugged her mother. "It was exactly right. And I have a dress that would be perfect on you, unless you'd rather spend the day shopping tomorrow."

"What about shoes?"

"We'll have to shop for those, and visit the hairdresser's— I'll call and make an appointment for you."

Lynette sat down on the bed. "Maybe I'm moving too fast. This is suddenly overwhelming."

"You can't back down now," Em said. "Why don't you have a relaxing cup of tea in the living room and read this ELLE magazine while we work?"

"Perhaps you're right," Lynette agreed and drifted out.

Em turned to Lucky and insisted on helping him, which both pleased and concerned him. They took measurements of the closet and discussed the needs for this room. Since it would become another guest bedroom when Em moved into her grandfather's room, she decided to add more shelf space for storage and less hanging space for clothes. Lucky drilled holes and cut the shelving to size while Em handed him tools and double-checked his measurements.

"This is fun," Em said. "I don't see many concrete results from the things I do. Teaching has rewards, but they're all intangible."

"If you're angling for a summer job redoing closets, I usually hire a couple of people. The pay is just above minimum wage." He picked up the screw gun, looked her over, and added, "For you, the benefits would make up for the low pay."

"That's bordering on sexual harassment. But, I'll call your bluff. What fringe benefits?"

"We do hang window shades with fringe if that's what the customer wants," Lucky said as he screwed in the brackets to hold down the shelves. "Other fringe benefits would include lunch with me every day, all the coffee you can drink, home-made ham biscuits each morning and tours of some of the finest homes in the High Country."

"Is that where you got some of the ideas you used building your house?"

"A few. Mostly I've known what that house would look like for a long time. If you like doing this type of work, you would have loved building that house." And he would have had her by his side all that time. "I've left room for expansion, by the way, in case you're volunteering."

"Would I still get the coffee and biscuits?"

Lucky grinned. "Grandma fixes those biscuits every morning. She'd gladly add another name to her list. I've thought about fitting Hambone with saddlebags so he can bring them to me hot out of the oven at six in the morning."

"She must get up at four!"

"She started that years ago when Grandpa was alive, and she's never changed. Back then, rumor has it, Grandpa had a liquor still somewhere on the property he gave to me. If that's true, he had to get up early to make the hour and a half drive to Spruce Pine."

"Was he a moonshiner?"

"No one ever proved it. I never found evidence of it, but that's what Uncle Harley said. I haven't had the heart to ask Grandma about it."

"Maybe that's what Grandfather's map is all about—a whisky still. Watauga County was dry until just a few years ago."

"When I told Grandma about you, she remembered an incident where your grandfather argued with mine. They were outside the courthouse in Boone. Grandma remembered it because it was unusual for Grandpa to get mad at anyone. He was an easy-going man unless his family was threatened somehow."

Maggie Bishop

"My grandfather had a low boiling point. He had to be in control of everyone."

Lucky cocked his head. "Are you suggesting that your grandfather and my grandpa were in business together? That's a little farfetched."

"You're right. I'd never heard the name Olin Tucker until I'd met you."

"Are you hinting for another trip to Spruce Pine soon?" Lucky asked as he put the last shelf in place.

"We could go this coming weekend."

Lucky grimaced. "I'll never finish all your closets at this rate. Let's move to your grandfather's closet so I can finish what I started yesterday."

By now, Em could anticipate which tools Lucky needed and they finished quickly. "What time should Uncle Harley and I pick up you ladies?" Lucky asked when they met with Lynette in the living room as he was leaving.

"Six-thirty, since it's a thirty-minute drive to Elk Creek Inn and cocktails are at seven. I know that's early, but this is rural America."

"And this country boy's going to be mighty hungry by eight when we eat."

"I'm sure they'll have appetizers," Em said, walking him to the door.

He paused and looked deeply into her eyes. "I know something I'd like to nibble on right now."

She tilted up her chin and he nibbled her lips. "That was just enough to whet my appetite." Em closed the door behind him and had a vision of him in a too-small, outdated suit. It didn't matter. She would go proudly with him however he was dressed.

~

Wednesday evening, Harley and Lucky, each wearing a dark blue suit, arrived at Em's house on time and were shown into the living room by the housekeeper. "I believe this suit shrunk since the last time I borrowed it. Bet it's tight on cousin Wes, too," Lucky said to his uncle when they were alone.

~79~

"Weight creeps up on you, if you're not careful. Before I went on that diet a while back, I'd gained only two pounds a year. It weren't no time til I was sixty pounds overweight and suffering for it. Losing it was no fun. Cut back on those morning biscuits."

"Not me. I'll slim down in the summer; I always do." Lucky let loose an appreciative whistle when Em walked into the living room in a form-fitting emerald green dress that ended far above her knees. Too far, if anyone wanted his opinion. Until now, all he'd seen her in were ski clothes and casual pants. The emerald pendant and emeralds hanging from her ears glistened. "Are you sure that dress is legal?" he asked as he walked around her to admire her from all angles.

"I have a license in my purse if you want to see it," came her smug reply.

Harley snickered.

"You're prettier than a sunrise over Grandfather Mountain," Lucky said.

"You can do better than that," said his uncle.

Lucky scowled and tried again. "You're prettier than a wild gobbler strutting his stuff."

Em was willing enough to let Lucky dig himself deeper into a hole, but her mother saved him by making her entrance.

Harley whistled long and slow, stopping Lynette in her tracks. Em took her hand and brought her forward where Harley presented his arm. "You're prettier than a whole row of gladiolus on a warm summer's day."

"Glads are my favorite flowers!" Lynette beamed at the praise as they walked out the door.

"Did you have your hair done? It's like a halo around your face," Harley said as he hooked her arm in his.

Lucky helped Em into her coat and grabbed Lynette's. When he caught up with the pair, he slid the coat over Lynette's shoulders. He doubted she even noticed.

~

When they arrived at the restaurant, Harley said to Lynette, "I don't want to let you out of my sight for fear one of these bucks will steal you away. If you were to hold on to my arm all night, I'd be a happy man."

Em looked at Lucky and they both knew that Lynette might make it through the evening after all.

The maitre d' led them upstairs to the private dining area where twenty people had gathered and milled about with drinks in their hands. The host introduced himself as Ed Johnson, then tried to pull Lynette aside, but she deferred to her daughter. As they walked away, Lucky overheard some of the schedule for the evening.

"A beer and two white wines," he said to the tuxedo-clad bartender. He rubbed his fingers along the rim of the cherry bar and glanced around the room. The men all looked like he expected stock brokers to look—dark suits, conservative hair cuts. The only man with long hair was the guy pouring the drinks and his was pulled back in a pony tail. Most of the women wore black long gowns. Em fairly shimmered in her green.

After Lucky joined the others with the drinks, the three of them stood around for a while. When no one talked to them, Lucky led them to a table where they would be more comfortable. This was Em's world and he was determined to enjoy it.

"Do you recognize anyone here?" Lucky asked Lynette. "Any of Mr. Graham's friends?"

She looked carefully around the room. "I didn't get involved with business activities. A few of these people came to visit him toward the end. I'm sorry that I don't know more."

Lucky could see that she grew more withdrawn with every passing minute. Em had abandoned them for a good thirty minutes, circulating in the room, playing the role of Everett Graham's granddaughter, when Lucky decided that the three of them would have their own party. "Did I ever tell you about the time Uncle Harley didn't want me to climb the tree to investigate a squirrel's nest, and I was just as determined to do it?"

Lynette tentatively shook her head and looked at Harley who groaned good-naturedly. "What happened?"

Lucky, like any good Southern storyteller, embellished the tale a bit. He managed to get Lynette to laugh aloud when he came to the part where Harley climbed the tree to get him. Harley's pants ripped to expose boxer shorts with hearts on them.

"What about the time you showed up at that party and three of your old girlfriends were there?" Harley asked.

"I'd be interested in hearing that one," Em said, finally joining them.

"Is everything okay?" Lucky asked, partly to deflect attention from that particular story.

"Yes. Ed started talking about stocks, and I couldn't get away any sooner. From the sound of the laughter over here, I'm missing all the fun. Everyone else keeps looking this way with envious glances. What about the three girlfriends?"

Lucky got hot under the collar and wanted to tear off the necktie. Stories about himself could be embarrassing.

"It seems," Harley began in a hushed voice, "they started comparing notes, and Lucky'd used the same lines on each one of them."

"I was only twenty at the time. I've wised up since then," Lucky interrupted.

"He'd even given them identical valentine cards."

"I didn't have time to pick out special ones—I had to get to work," Lucky explained.

"When the girls found out that the necklaces he'd given them matched, they had to get revenge."

Lucky kept quiet. Anything he could add would only make it worse.

"First, they took off the necklaces which they'd been wearing close to their hearts, filed by him, and dropped them one at a time into his drink. That wasn't the worst . . ." Harley took a drink of his wine to build the suspense.

"Then they play-acted out his sweetest lines in front of everyone."

"It was months before I could get another date," Lucky interjected. "When I'd call up a girl, all she'd do was laugh. To this day, women will still approach me and say 'you smell prettier than bacon frying in a cast iron skillet,' laugh in my face, then walk away."

Lynette and Em giggled like teenagers.

Ed asked everyone to be seated and told a few stories about Everett Graham's success in stocks. He joked about this party being a tax write-off for his corporation. Lucky tuned out after a while and put his arm on the back of Em's dinner chair. Her hair was pulled up, exposing her long, slender neck. The drop earrings were three emeralds in a row lined in silver. Her feathered bangs ended at her eyebrows and he thought her eyes were the prettiest he'd ever seen—not that he would ever use 'prettiest' in her presence again.

". . . and in 1973, Everett managed to sell his stocks just before the bottom dropped out. While it took the rest of us a decade to recover, he kept right on going. His reputation was built that year. Since he was the founder of the Stock Club thirty years ago, we honor his memory with this plaque. His daughter-in-law, Lynette Graham, will accept."

Lynette's startled eyes turned to Em who urged her on. Her simple "Thank you" was enough speech for the occasion. Harley held her shaking hand after she sat back down.

"Mother, before you say anything, I want you to know that I thought he was going to call me," Em said.

"You looked beautiful up there," Harley said.

"Where are you going to hang the plaque?" Lucky asked. "I'll put it up on my next trip over."

"I don't know. Probably the library," Lynette said, her gaze focused on Harley.

At that point, the waiters brought out the appetizers and placed small tongs above the plate. Lucky picked up his fork and moved one of the four shells in front of him, then stared intently at it. "Are these what I think they are?"

Em, holding the opened tong in her left hand, inserted a tiny fork inside the shell and lifted out the meat. "Escargot. Snails in garlic. I love these things."

He watched her slip the morsel into her mouth. He almost envied the little critter.

"I'm so hungry I'd eat a fried frog," Harley said as he imitated Em's method. "M-m-m, that's good."

To Lucky's surprise, the meat was firm, not gooey, and had a subtle flavor. "These must be expensive since they only gave us four each. I'll bet they want you to save room for the main course," he said.

Next came a tiny bowl of broth with a few slivers of vegetables floating in it, followed by a salad.

"Isn't this lovely?" Lynette asked, admiring the way the two cucumber slices were arranged next to two red bell pepper slices.

"Yes it is," Harley answered, eyes only for her.

By the time the entree was served, Lucky's stomach growled. He politely asked for more rolls and another beer as the waiter removed the empty plates. "What are we having next?" Lucky asked Em.

"Lamb in mint sauce," she said as a plate was set in front of her. "Such attention to detail," she exclaimed to Lucky. Each of the four medallions lay side by side with the sauce carefully ladled over them. "The touch of mint, see, adds just the right color as well as taste. Eat," she said when Lucky simply stared at his sparsely-covered plate. He saw more plate than food.

He cut one medallion in half, ate it, and repeated the motion. The texture wasn't that different from beef, but the flavor was strange. "It's good, exotic like you promised." He leaned over and quietly asked Em, "Is this all there is?"

At first, she looked puzzled, then nodded. "I'm afraid so."

Lucky cleaned his plate in two seconds flat, including the three new potatoes, ate the rolls, then settled back with a cup of coffee. "No wonder the French are so skinny, if this is a regular meal."

"I should have warned you that they serve small portions of delicious food."

"After eight hours of skiing, I need big portions." He suddenly realized that he was making the women uncomfortable. "Don't mind me. They'll have dessert, right?"

"Of course."

When the waiter set a sliver of pie in front of him, he looked up and met three sets of eyes looking at him. Em giggled first, then Lynette, and finally Harley laughed.

"With that hangdog expression, you look like Hambone being offered a soy burger."

"Don't laugh. I know you're still hungry," Lucky said to Harley.

"I'm not thirty and still growing. This has been an excellent experience. Thank you, Lynette, for inviting me."

"It's been a pleasure."

"I'm sure we'll pass an open fast food place on the way home," Em said to Lucky.

"If I don't starve to death first," he teased.

~

Lynette and Harley said goodnight at the door while Em and Lucky kissed in the back seat of the car. "Mmm. Now that is one French custom I approve of," Lucky said, as they came apart for air.

Chapter 9

By noon the next day, Em was eager to get to Sugar Mountain for her third day of skiing. Weather reports called for more snow, but she wasn't worried, thanks to chains in the trunk of her Audi. Besides, more snow, fresh powder, was every skier's dream.

The light gray cloud cover stayed with her on the thirty-minute drive from the University. After parking her car, she went directly to the line at the bottom of the yellow lift, confidently stepped into her ski bindings and scanned the area for a certain red-jacketed ski patroller.

"Have you seen Lucky?" she asked the lift operator as he motioned her forward into position to catch the chair.

"He went up about twenty minutes ago," the operator said as she rose into the air for her ride to the top. No red jackets were visible at the base of the slope, and soon she looked down on the tops of evergreens. The trail passed under the lift and she spotted a ski patroller helping a downed skier. The accident couldn't have been serious since the patroller helped the skier to his feet. Back above the woods, deer tracks lingered in the snow near the creek.

The last stretch on the lift was steeper; the trees below stunted by wind. "Hoarfrost," she whispered upon seeing the hard white crystals on the branches. A gray squirrel high-tailed it across the snow, up a tree trunk and didn't pause until it was safely on a branch. Its tail twitched the whole time it took her chair to pass. The lift slowed and stopped. Silence hung in the cold air, a silence so complete she was sure the world was at peace. Overhead the clear deep Carolina blue sky had a couple of short-lived contrails. To the west, a line of dark clouds seemed hung up on the Tennessee mountain tops.

She negotiated the exit ramp and skied to the right edge of the intermediate slope, then stopped and looked out over the valley below and across to the next mountain. The roads wound like ribbons threaded through lace. House rooftops were barely visible through leafless trees on the other mountain and, here and there, caches of snow blazed bright white.

Looking directly down, she gulped as two women skied by her, poling to pick up speed. One of these days, she thought, she'd be that good a skier. If she didn't give it up at the end of the season like she had every other sport she tried. Maybe this time she'd have reason to keep up with it.

All traces of the early morning slope grooming were gone but the snow was still smooth. Em had no trouble turning left, then right, then left again within the slope boundaries. She kept turning to keep down her speed and tried to remember to always point her chest down the hill, keep her weight on the balls of her feet, and not to cross her skis.

Even with frequent stops, she hadn't spotted Lucky. About half way down, she saw a male patroller standing close to a woman so she headed that way to get a better look. It was him —with a woman skier.

Drat, just her luck to be caught conspicuously running after him by a witness, and a pretty one at that. Here she was, after knowing a guy only two weeks and sharing a few kisses with him, jealous because he looked down on another woman's face and they laughed together.

Miffed at herself, Em decided to change course so he wouldn't see her. Without looking ahead, she blindly turned into a snow bump, a mogul as Lucky called it. She dipped into it at the same moment she shifted her weight.

Suddenly she was airborne and screaming. Seconds later, both skis hit the snow, hard. Her knees buckled, which turned out to be a good thing because she kept her balance and skidded to a halt. Her heart thudded in her chest. Looking up, she found Lucky standing directly in front of her. She gulped.

"Very impressive, don't you think, Suzanne?" Lucky asked.

"Good show," the woman beside him commented.

"Some patrollers would call that reckless skiing," Lucky continued, talking to the other woman.

"But no one was hurt," came Suzanne's defense.

"What would you call it, Em? Reckless, out of control, or involuntary," Lucky asked.

Em noted the twinkle in his eyes. "What's the difference?"

"The wrong answer will cost you your lift ticket."

"But this is a season ticket." Em glanced at the other woman who nodded sagely.

"Could you do it again?"

"No, never, nada. It was an accident. Honest." Em reminded herself of her own students.

"Next time, be more careful. You could hurt yourself or someone else. See you later, Lucky," Suzanne said, and she skied off.

Em looked down at the snow, not sure what to say to Lucky now that she'd found him.

"That was my cousin Wes' wife." Lucky nodded down the slope before he looked back at Em. "It was the blood-curling scream that gave you away. Had it been a deliberate act and a whoop for joy, I would have had to rip your ticket in half." Lucky's eyes sparkled the way she remembered them. "The jump looked good—graceful form, clean landing, steady balance. Like a ballet dancer."

"You say the sweetest things," Em cooed, leaning into him for effect, then promptly fell down.

After he'd helped her back up, they skied some runs together, with Em improving all the time. They stopped on the slope to enjoy the big, fat snow flakes drifting down in the gentle wind.

Within five minutes the wind swirled around them and the snow turned to small, piercing dots. Lucky told Em, "This is turning wicked. We'll be in the middle of a cloud soon so I suggest you go on in while you can still see." The wind had picked up and visibility diminished as they spoke.

"Your shift's almost over. Will you join me for a drink in the lounge?" Em said.

"Only if you've finished skiing for the day. I've taken down too many inebriated skiers in the sled to encourage you to imbibe as you slide."

"I've skied enough today. My legs won't hold out much longer."

"I'll meet you in half an hour. The lounge is on the third floor."

By the time Em reached the bottom, more than just her knees shook. The fog socked in the slope. She skied the second half of the mountain almost inch by inch. She kept her eyes open wide to use her peripheral vision to detect other skiers, but even the schussing sound of skiers passing her was muffled. At the bottom, after what felt like hours, her hands trembled as she locked her skis in the rental ski stand. She made her way into the lodge to her gear locker and changed from the stiff and awkward-on-dry-land ski boots to regular walking boots.

"Sorry I'm late," Lucky said an hour later when he sat at Em's table beside a window in the lounge. She sure looked warm and relaxed compared to his own rushed state. "I had to answer a call. A guy fell and dislocated his clavicle on this side," he said, pointing to his neck. "It normally sits in a hollow in the sternum."

"Does the doctor pop it back in like they do for a dislocated shoulder?"

"No, sometimes they let it float. Too many nerves, muscles and arteries are jammed in that area of the neck for it to be reattached. Then it took the ambulance longer than usual to get here." Lucky took a long gulp of beer, happy that she'd waited for him and thrilled to be near her again, even though they'd been separated only a short time.

"Your beer's probably warm by now."

"It's fine," he said, staring out the window. "It looks like somebody threw a white sheet across the glass. You can't see two feet in front of you out there."

"It was bad enough when I came down."

"The updated weather report is calling for thirty inches of snow tonight. This morning they said it would be three to four inches. Storm must have stalled above us. Are you in a hurry to get home?"

She shook her head. "It's too late for that. I called Mother, and she said Boone has had six inches since noon. Accidents have temporarily closed Highway 105. I might as well stay here and try later."

"No sane person would drive in this." Lucky peeled down part of the bottle label with his thumb nail. "Here are your options. There are condos beside the slopes. I'm sure they'll rent one for a single night, considering the circumstances." He took a swallow of beer from the bottle, giving her time to think about it. "Or you could stay with me."

"I couldn't put you out like that."

"I think I have the fixings for spaghetti," he added. Since she'd liked his pizza so well, she'd love his spaghetti—he used the same sauce.

"What about my 10:00 class tomorrow?"

"We'll listen to the school cancellation and delay reports early in the morning. I'll check with Uncle Harley tonight. He has a scanner so he'll tell us about the blocked roads. Getting out of Sugar won't be much trouble; they plow the roads constantly. Avery County's tax base *is* the ski slopes so they'll keep the roads open. It's Boone that's the problem."

"I don't have any clothes or a toothbrush . . ."

"Borrow my clothes. And I have spare toothbrushes. Every time I visit the dentist for a cleaning they give me extras. You'll be safe and warm in front of my fire."

Lucky looked out the window to give her a moment to make up her mind, watching her reflection on the snow-white background. He wouldn't wonder where she was or what she was doing as had become his habit of late. There couldn't be a better way to start the day than to see her face first thing in the morning.

"I'll do it," Em said.

"Hambone'll be happy. He gets bored with just me around in the evenings."

They left the warmth and lights of the lodge and headed out into the haunting white of the snow cloud sitting on the mountain.

"We'll ride up the yellow lift and walk from there." By the time they reached the top and jogged away from the lift, snow fall had dropped visibility to an island of thirty feet around them. They left the slopes quickly and followed a trail that skirted some cliffs. Lucky held onto her hand, partly to steady her over the unseen rocks underfoot, partly so he wouldn't lose her in the diffused light, but mainly because he wanted to. Even through their glove-covered hands, the pressure of her grasp stirred up his insides.

The snow clung to her hat and fell softly onto her jacket. Lucky didn't bother dusting her off; she was like a little snow bunny. He stopped and tugged at her hand. Her cold lips melted against his as he hugged her close. The wind swirled around them, urging them to keep moving. Tree branches drooped from the weight of the wet snow. All was quiet except for the crunch of their boots. After twenty minutes of steady walking through the trees in deep snow, she hadn't complained or flagged a bit through that ordeal, he thought.

Not at all what he'd expect from a rich woman. Lucky whistled a high, loud, piercing whistle. Moments later, Hambone bounded out of the white cloud and barked at his feet.

"Good dog, Hambone," Lucky said, kneeling down to the dog's eye level and scratching behind his ears. "Lead us home," he commanded, taking Em's hand and following closely behind the happy heap of fur.

"Do you have to walk home like this often?"

"A few times each ski season. We get plenty of whiteouts, but the snow's not usually this heavy. The Farmer's Almanac is calling for this storm to be one for the record books. So far, that's more accurate than the TV."

"How big?" Em asked as they stepped onto his front deck.

"It says we'll get fifty, but the radio is calling for only twenty to twenty-four inches." He used his boot as a shovel to clear a space in the snow and opened the door to let them into the warm house. He dropped his hat and gloves in a heap in a corner of the kitchen.

"My vote's with the radio prediction," Em said, brushing the snow from her jacket.

"We'll know which one is right come morning. Here, let me take your coat." His gaze lingered on a drop of melted snow dangling at the tip of her ear. Kiss it away, he thought, and would have done so if she hadn't moved to shrug out of her coat. "I'll start a fire in a jiffy."

Chapter 10

On her way to the living room, Em was distracted by the hall bookshelf. She pulled down a battered paperback, well-used, as they all seemed from the cracked spines. There was a used bookstore stamp inside the cover. Imagine having to buy used paperbacks, she thought. They were so inexpensive brand new.

The books were arranged by subject. The medical shelves were stuffed and overflowing to the floor. Detective novels, dog training manuals, house construction, westerns, war, physics, astronomy, philosophy . . . who would have guessed that the rugged man had such an inquiring mind. A jock with a brain. A local not restricted by latitude. Her own collection of books were leather-bound to fit the decor.

One title laying on top of a stack on the floor stopped her musing. *How To Marry Rich.* A cold stillness came over her. "Be aware," her grandfather had often said, "money attracts. It's magnetic. You will face the dollar dilemma when it comes to men." How right he'd been in her early college years. Did people pay attention to her only because of what they could gain? How could she ever be sure she was valued for herself, apart from her wealth? Without money, who am I?

Shaking herself to cast off the unwelcome thoughts, Em wandered into the basically empty living room and looked around, evaluating the possibilities in furnishing the space. It could be done in either fine antiques or contemporary leather. The English cottage look with chintz would go well with the exterior, she thought, her footsteps echoing in the large room as she crossed the hardwood floor to the couch in front of the fireplace.

"I'll build the fire if you like," Em offered in a voice loud enough to carry back to the kitchen.

"I'll coach you," Lucky said, bringing in two steaming mugs. "Hot chocolate."

"How did you do that so fast?" she asked, taking a proffered mug.

"Microwave. I don't suppose you use one, do you?"

"Martha considers the kitchen her domain. If I don't eat with her, I eat out. I'm afraid that domestic training was not part of my education. Grandfather always said that I could hire help, and that it was part of my duty to provide work for others."

"My philosophy has always been to learn to do it myself. As long as I'm capable and willing, I should be able to take care of most things that come up. Why pay when I don't have to?"

"Why *do* when I can hire someone to do it for me?" Em countered partly for the effect, not completely believing or living that philosophy.

Lucky's eyes narrowed. "You're joshing. You don't really feel that way." At her raised eyebrow, he asked, "Why do you work? You could spend your days at the spa or shopping."

"My, my. You have a warped vision of those with money. I work for many of the same reasons you do." Em saw the doubt in his eyes. "Not to pay the bills, of course. But to help, to make a difference. You save bodies—I save minds."

"Does that mean you take back the offer to build the fire?" Lucky asked, between sips of hot chocolate.

Em laughed and shook her head. "It'll be fun."

Following his instructions, she flicked the lighter under the kindling. It flared up and caught the narrow sticks on fire. After a few moments, she added a piece of poplar, then locust in the front, and stacked another piece of oak on top of the kindling.

"You realize, of course," he said after they'd washed their hands, "that you have to add pieces of wood periodically to keep the fire going."

Em sat down on the opposite end of the sofa. "I've already figured that out. You're a thorough teacher."

He laid one arm on the back, and she wished she'd sat closer to him. She put her hand on the back of the sofa, meeting his fingers.

Lucky emptied the last of the chocolate from his mug and set it on the floor, stretching so he wouldn't break contact with her fingers.

"I'm thorough in whatever I do," he said huskily, interlocking their hands and sliding closer to her.

"I'll bet when you were a kid you took apart the riding lawn mower and put it back together just to see how it worked." She squeezed his fingers.

"We didn't have a lawn mower, but I did dismantle the tractor one time. It took me a week to get it running again. Dad was hopping mad. I thought I'd never be able to sit down again."

Em had the grace to be embarrassed by her presumption.

"We had a goat to keep the grass down, what little there was. Since we lived in the woods, a lawn didn't fit—like a cat on a huntin' trip."

"I see," she said quietly. Obviously she had a lot to learn about this man and his life.

"I don't know about you, but I'm hungry. Are you ready for another coaching session?"

"I've seen a pasta machine before, but I have no idea how to use one," she said in all seriousness.

Lucky shook his head. "We'll use boxed pasta and bottled sauce, doctored up a little."

Cheap ingredients, poor results Martha was fond of saying. She could always go easy on the sauce and fill up on the pasta.

He took her hand and led her to the kitchen where he tied a towel around her waist. "I don't have an apron, but this'll keep your clothes clean."

"I thought all good cooks wore aprons."

"This cook doesn't. If you'll fill this pot," he said, taking one from the cabinet, "with cold water and put it on the large front burner, I'll open the wine."

"Wine?" Em set the pot in the sink and turned on the water. "I thought you only drank beer."

"Figured it was time I expanded my horizons a bit," Lucky set a bottle and two glasses on the counter. "The fellow at Peabody's said this was 'complex and spicy'. It's Mer—lot."

"It's pronounced Mer—*lo*. It's French." Em laughed, then sobered at his stricken look. "Don't get upset. I think it's wonderful you bought wine. And you even got the right glasses."

"You mean you have to have different glasses for different kinds of wine? These were just the ones the fellow at Peabody's sold me."

"Well, yes. White wine glasses are taller than those; then champagne glasses can be flutes, or—"

"The water—"

"Oh!"

The pot was overflowing and threatening to inundate the kitchen. Em turned off the water but it was still so full that it sloshed when she picked it up. She put it on the burner then studied the knobs and discovered tiny diagrams indicating the appropriate controls for each burner. Since it was a gas stove, she looked around for matches.

Lucky poured the wine into the glasses and then watched Em search for a moment before he explained that it had an automatic pilot. He dumped some of the water out of the pot and covered it. "This is how you boil water," he said with a straight face.

"We must start with the basics," Em said with an equally straight face. He showed her how to defrost the meat in the microwave, brown the venison and cook chopped onion in the same pan, add the spaghetti sauce, cook the pasta, and dish it out. All without spilling a drop on her clothes or on the towel. She now knew how to fix two meals, she thought. At this rate, her housekeeper might soon have a rival in the kitchen.

The wind howled outside the house. "Does that mean the storm's getting worse?" Em peered into the dark outside the window.

"Not necessarily, but it'll snow all night."

She looked up at the ceiling, wondering how much snow the roof could hold.

"Are you questioning my construction skills?"

"No," she said too quickly and didn't look at him.

"Dinner's ready."

Em gingerly took a bite. She swallowed and blurted out, "It's fine!"

Lucky held up his glass. "Here's to Em's first solo cooking experience. May they all turn out as good."

Em grinned when she tapped his glass with hers. "I had no idea cooking was so much fun. No wonder Martha won't let me near her kitchen—she's afraid I'll take over her job."

After dinner, Lucky showed her how to stack the dishes in the dishwasher before they returned to the living room.

"Your turn to poke the fire," Lucky said. He patted the spot next to him, then he held her. They discussed food, books, movies and work. Em snuggled closer to him when he talked about serious accidents and laughed aloud when he described his early attempts at snowboarding. She gazed at the fire and basked in his company while Hambone sprawled across the floor next to the hearth. Lucky looked down at Hambone. "You want your tummy scratched, don't you?"

"Is that under the heading of foreplay?"

"Do you think it will work?" They both leaned down and scratched the animal.

"I need to check on my grandmother. Is there anyone you need to call?" Lucky asked, obviously reluctant to let go of their quiet time together.

"Oh my gosh. I forgot to call Mother!" Em exclaimed and took the phone Lucky offered, and punched in the numbers.

"I'm fine, Dear. Harley brought me home from the hospital and offered to stay," Lynette said, "but I hate to impose. And, how would it look to the neighbors?"

"Mother, the family reputation can use a little gossip. Even nosy neighbors take a break during a snow storm. Is it safe for Harley to drive home?" Em asked.

"I doubt it."

"That answers your question. He has to stay and it can all be explained to the neighbors later. Besides, I think you're attracted to him. Take this opportunity to get to know him better," Em said, conscious that Lucky sat next to her.

"This is all so new to me. I'm not sure I can entertain a man all evening. What will we talk about?"

"You could play cards or dominos. That way, you can talk when you feel like it, but you won't be compelled to fill in the silence."

"I'll do that. Oh, I almost forgot. The accountant called and set up an appointment for Tuesday. I hope you enjoy your stay with Lucky."

"I'm sure I will. I'll call you tomorrow." Em hung up the phone. "Your Uncle Harley's either a very kind man or a very bold rascal."

"He's a little of both, like all the Tuckers. Maybe he's just what your mother needs."

After Lucky checked on his grandmother, he tilted up Em's chin and looked into her eyes. "Are you going to call me a rascal for doing this?" and he kissed her. His first kiss was gentle, in keeping with the evening.

His next one was deeper and pulsated with desire. She fairly melted in his arms. A log on the fire crackled and the heat radiated out to them. His lips warmed hers and her heart beat loudly in her ears. Do I want to make love with him? her mind asked. Oh yes, her body answered.

To her dismay, he ended the kiss. His voice cracked when he whispered, "Where do you want to sleep?"

She hesitated.

"I understand. It's too soon for you. Don't worry. I can sleep out here on the couch."

She blinked in puzzlement. "But—"

His finger over her lips silenced her. "Don't make this any harder than it already is. I promised you a safe place to stay."

Em sighed. "You said you have a spare bedroom."

"I do, but no furniture."

"You may be a rascal in thought, but you're a knight in deed," she said, releasing him.

His arm around her, he walked her to the bedroom door, only to stub his toe on a pile of books. "The stacks on the floor are going to RAMs Rack, as soon as I get around to it. Sometimes I buy a table full of books at an estate sale, then donate the ones I don't want."

"Good idea." Emerald nodded with a sudden smile.

He left her at his bedroom door after giving her one of his tee shirts to sleep in. It would be a long night. Add honorable to the list of his attributes. She doubted she'd be as noble, were their roles reversed.

~

Lucky opened his eyes early the next morning in the bright stillness and walked to the door to let out Hambone. At least three feet of snow greeted them on the deck and Hambone tried to retreat back into the house. Lucky shoved him out and shut the door. He started the coffee maker then returned to the living room to turn on the TV and check the weather forecast. All he got was a typed message on the bottom of the screen: "Searching for satellite."

"What's going on?" came a sleepy inquiry from the kitchen.

Lucky swung around, startled at the noise, and his mouth went slack at the sight of Em, hair disheveled and eyes only partly opened. She was clothed in only his tee shirt, her breasts pressed against the cotton, and he could make out the dark circles formed by her nipples. The tail of his shirt brushed her thighs well above the knees.

"I smelled the coffee," Em said.

"Coming right up," he said, dragging his gaze away from her. "Are you up for a quick adventure?"

"Now?"

"After a cup of coffee. I need someone to hold the ladder while I climb up on the roof."

Em walked to the door and looked out. "In this?" The trunks of trees were buried in snow. Shrubs around the house had disappeared into undulating blankets of white.

"My little eighteen-inch satellite dish must be covered with it. I'm not getting a picture. All I have to do is brush off the snow and then we can check the weather report," Lucky said, walking to her. "You're cute as a kitten this morning." Lucky restricted himself to a kiss on her forehead before reaching for two coffee cups.

When his back was to her, she hugged him from behind. "Thanks for keeping me safe last night."

"Bringing you here was easy. Leaving you alone in my bed wasn't," he said gruffly, relishing the feel of her against his back and her arms around his waist.

He filled the cups, and they sat on two stools at the kitchen counter quickly drinking the brew and quietly staring at the snow. After they dressed in ski clothes, complete with hat and gloves, Lucky retrieved the extension ladder from the garage. Em carried the back end, and Lucky led them around to the far side of the house. Walking was difficult because each step involved lifting the foot as high as possible then pushing forward through the snow before putting the foot down. Lucky, in effect, pushed out a path for them.

"I didn't realize part of the house was underground."

"The master bath and the closet to the guest bedroom are built into the side of the mountain. It saves on heating and cooling," he explained as he sank one end of the ladder deep into the snow then let the other end fall against the snow-covered roof.

"Do you want to come up with me? You can stay on the ladder so you don't slip while I make my way over to the dish."

"Of course. What kind of an adventure would it be for me

if I stayed down here?"

"Let me get to the top before you come up," Lucky said, carefully stepping onto a rung. Sinking the toe of his boot into the snow, he pushed against the rung and climbed. He called from the tip of the roof, "It's easy, come on up."

He watched her climb the ladder with a small smile that grew into a grin with each of her steps. At the top of the ladder, she sat in the snow and looked around. The clouds high above the mountain across the valley had tinges of pink, signaling the sunrise. Fir trees nearby were bent over, laden with snow. Here and there chimney smoke made dark traces against the stark white snow-covered mountains. The road was impossible to discern.

"I have to be at work in an hour. Are you up for fresh powder skiing?"

"After I call to make sure the college is closed for the day."

"This is slick," Lucky cautioned, standing on the steep roof incline. "There must be a layer of ice under all this snow." He knelt in the snow and shuffled forward on his hands and knees. When he reached the stand to the dish, he brushed the snow off with his hand, careful not to bang any of the surface. The trip back to the ladder was easier since he'd already cleared the path, but his knee slipped out from under him.

He had nowhere to go but down.

Chapter 11

Lucky tried to grab something to stop his slide down the roof. Nothing worked. Faster he went, hardly hearing his own "Whoa!"

He ran out of roof, sailed two feet past the edge, through the air and into the snow bank with a dull thud. Stunned, he sat peering out of the hole he had punched in the eye level snowbank for several blank seconds.

"Lucky, are you hurt?" Em called.

"Hell, no!" he roared. "That was great!"

"My turn," she shouted. She scooted over beside the ladder and let go. "Wheeee," she cried all the way down. She landed next to him, making a heart-shaped hole.

Lucky laughed and helped her stand. There was a mad scramble to the ladder. Em won. Lucky climbed up behind her, admiring the view.

She jumped right while he jumped left. They slid, hitting

bottom at the same time. Hambone joined them, adding barks and face licks to the ruckus.

"One more time?" Em asked.

"Last one up cooks breakfast," he challenged, jumping to the third rung to get ahead of her.

"No fair. You had a head start! You knew what you were going to say," she yelled, scrambling to catch up with him.

"In the interest of time, we'll share the cooking." He reached for her hand and sat beside her. They slid down together, laughing all the way.

~

"I'm starved," Em said after they put away the ladder, shed their outer garments, and had another cup of coffee in front of them.

The TV weather forecast reported that the storm had dumped snow all up and down the Appalachian Mountain range from upper Virginia down into Georgia, with the heaviest concentrations in North Carolina. "It looks like another great weekend for Sugar Mountain. People from Florida will flock up here."

"Will they be able to open the roads in time?" Em asked.

"The road crews probably worked all night. The main road will be open by now. What'll it be—eggs and bacon, waffles, or cold cereal?"

"Waffles."

Lucky took a frozen pack from the freezer and tossed it to her. "You toast these in the toaster oven while I nuke the syrup." In moments, jam and butter were on the table and a stack of ten waffles steamed on a plate. "How hungry are you?" Lucky asked, eyeing the waffles.

"I had so much fun using the toaster oven that I may have been carried away. Can we eat all of those?"

"If we can't, Hambone'll eat the leftovers. Grandma made the blueberry jam. Sometimes I like to use that instead of butter and syrup."

Em tried it then smiled from earring to earring. "Your grandmother definitely has culinary talent. I wonder how hard it is to make jam?"

"Not hard but time-consuming. It involves standing over a hot stove. I definitely won't be teaching you how to do that." He pushed his chair back. "We'd better clean up, then I got to get to work."

The trip in the deep snow down to the top of the lift was difficult but uneventful. In the shadows of the lodge, he kissed her, lingering as long as he dared.

"I wish we could have spent the day at your place," she said, echoing his thoughts.

"I have bills to pay."

"Let's not forget that you love to ski," she added.

As they'd arranged, Lucky met her at the bottom of the yellow lift at nine-fifteen, and they rode up together. "How is skiing in powder different from the way I've been skiing?" Em asked him.

"You need to keep your weight further back to the middle of your foot to keep the ski tips up. Turns have to be more gradual since the edges don't do much in this snow. Plus, you won't see the skis. Let's get off at Mid and turn right to the beginner's slope."

"I'm demoted?"

"Only until you get the feel for this. Powder gives you a weightless, floating sensation, like flying without wings. You'll want to use the parallel turn we practiced, and establish a rhythm so you can link one turn with the next. Always—and I mean always—start the turn by going straight down the hill, then bank left or right."

"Straight down the hill?" she said faintly.

"We're on the beginners' slope. You'll probably have more trouble keeping moving than anything else. This stuff slows you down."

"Anything else?"

"Exaggerate your up-and-down knee movements."

"How am I supposed to remember all of this? You're frightening me."

Caught by surprise, he paused. "I'll talk you through it. Follow me off the ramp and head right." He raised the safety bar to dismount. When he was past the bottom, he turned to find Em down in the deep snow at the base of the ramp. He held his breath.

"It's a good thing I taped my knee this morning," Em grumbled. She used her poles to stand up. She skied the rest of the day without mishap and improved with each run. Lucky responded to injury calls, managing to ski with her off and on all day. It was against policy, but he figured he'd bend the rules just this once. Other patrollers waved, but no one complained.

"The road to Boone is clear," Lucky told her when they met in the lodge after his last run of the day.

"I guess that means I'll sleep in my own bed tonight," Em said.

He took her hands in his. "You're more than welcome to stay in mine."

Her eyes widened, then twinkled. "What would your neighbors say?"

The glow on her face as she looked up at him took his breath away. "That I'm a lucky man to have such a good-lookin', accomplished and smart woman staying with me."

"Do you think that about me?"

" 'Course, even if it's a little late in your life to be learning how to cook." Lucky said. "I'll call you."

As she went to her car and he went into the patrol room, he felt as though he was parting from someone very important to him. It struck him as odd because they had only known each other for two weeks.

~

Monday evening Em just happened to drop by his house; she couldn't make it until Wednesday to see him again. "I brought Hambone a present," she said. The wide collar had been hand-tooled at a leather shop.

"You didn't have to do that," Lucky protested as he put it around the big dog's neck.

"Yeah, I know. Doesn't he look handsome?" Em stroked

Hambone's ear then reached into the bag. "These are for you. I wanted to get you some new ski boots but the salesclerk insisted that you had to try them on."

Lucky frowned and hesitated before reaching for them. "It don't feel right—you buyin' me things."

"They're just ski gloves."

"You're making me nervous. I don't have anything to give you."

"I just wanted to give you something. I can afford it."

"That *really* makes me feel good."

"You're taking this the wrong way." Then she realized that she'd dented his ego. His lack of money was unimportant to her, but it apparently mattered to him. "Hey," she said, wrapping her arms around him, "let's not fight about this. I can only stay a minute so let's not waste it." She kissed him and ended up staying for an hour.

~

Tuesday afternoon, Em managed to arrive at the accountant's office on time, even though she'd had to cut short an appointment with one of her students.

"Have a seat. Would you like some coffee?" Bill Adler asked in a tight voice.

A nervous accountant. Not a good sign. She declined the coffee and sat on the edge of her seat. He sat on the other side of a cluttered desk, almost as if he wanted the sturdy barrier between them.

"I apologize for not calling you earlier, but Everett left explicit instructions not to bother you with details."

"Details like failing to pay the electric bill?" Her grip tightened on the purse in her lap.

"I apologize for that oversight also. Lynette asked me to continue in the same capacity the day after he died. I called her and tried to tell her some of the details of his will."

When she had asked her mother about finances, Lynette had said she had it under control. She'd told Em not to worry about it. There would be time later, after Em was resettled at home, for her to take over the finances. These past few months, Em had been too busy with a new teaching position, too involved in learning to ski. It felt too much like prying.

Bill sighed and his pinched face paled before he spoke again. "Your grandfather was not the shrewd investor he had led everyone to believe. Then his medical bills depleted most of the second mortgage money."

"Second mortgage? He told me a long time ago that the house was paid for." *If this man has been playing fast and loose with my estate money . . .* She didn't finish the thought.

Bill fumbled through the papers in a thick folder. "Yes, that was true. It was paid off briefly in 1998. See," he said, eagerly pointing to the physical proof.

Em grabbed the papers from his hand. The house had been debt free, but a mortgage for six hundred thousand dollars had been taken out six months later. The papers showed that this was eighty percent of its appraised value. Her eyes pinned the accountant to his chair. "What happened to all his money?"

Bill swallowed and tugged at the cuff of his shirt sleeve. "He worked hard to repay that mortgage. The stock market wasn't cooperating but he'd managed to whittle it down when he had his stroke."

"Cut to the bottom line." Em's stomach muscles tightened as far as they could go. Her throat practically closed up at his evasion of her question.

"Your estate is depleted. You are deeply in debt and I'm at my wit's end in coming up with ideas to pull you out of it."

She glared at him. "Why didn't you tell me this when Grandfather died?"

"He ordered it. I was to protect the family at all costs."

At first, she couldn't believe what she heard. If her grandfather had felt that way, he wouldn't have meant for things to get this far out of hand.

"After his stroke, Everett left explicit instructions for me."

That much she knew was true. "What went wrong with his plan?"

"My fiduciary duty as executor of the estate was to follow the deceased's instructions to the letter. My first act was to preserve the estate so I liquidated immediately. Lynette agreed. It wasn't my fault that the market rose in all stocks but those he'd bought."

Em narrowed her eyes at his sudden change to calling her grandfather "deceased" instead of the first name as he'd used moments ago. "How long did you plan to keep this from me?"

"I was instructed to shield the family from financial problems. You were never to know. Lynette knew."

The man shrank before her. Her world was crumbling but she couldn't blame him entirely. Her grandfather had been notorious for bending people to his will. "How much do you get for being the accountant?"

"One thousand dollars a month."

Although his answer was barely audible, it thundered in Em's head. Twelve thousand dollars a year to write checks was outrageous, especially now. Why had Grandfather retained this man who was obviously not that competent? "I'm taking all the expense files with me." She stood and barely reined in her anger as she grabbed the folders. "Your services are no longer needed. Contact the necessary businesses for a change in billing addresses. Immediately."

~

Em went through the motions of driving home, eating dinner, and kissing her mother goodbye as Lynette left on yet another date with Harley. All the while, Em tried to accept what she had heard hours ago. Once the house was quiet, she entered her grandfather's study and closed the door behind her.

"It can't be true," she whispered. "Tell me this is a nightmare, and I'll wake up in a few minutes."

The steady tick of the old Grandfather clock in the corner was her only answer. She walked around the room and looked at the many framed photographs of her grandfather shaking hands with important people, speaking before civic groups, holding her hand on her eleventh birthday. The photos reminded her that his clothes had always been top quality, and he had spent lavishly on her, especially since her mother had never paid much attention to shopping.

Eventually, she made her way to his desk and to the folder she'd placed on it earlier. For long moments, she stared at the manila folder, afraid to touch it for fear the contact would make the accountant's words come true.

Once she opened the folder, it didn't take long for the gist of the information to come clear. Bill Adler hadn't lied.

She banged her fist on the desk. "I don't deserve this," she said aloud. I hate him, she thought. I hated fighting him when he was alive and hate his secrecy now that he's dead.

She flew around the room, ripping the photos off the wall. "Fiduciary duty!" Crash! Into the trash can. "Estate depleted!" Certificates and honorary plaques hit the can, too. She wanted to wipe the place clean, eliminate all traces of Everett Graham. If he were standing in front of her, she'd sock him in the nose.

But he wasn't, she realized as her anger played itself out. Returning to the chair, she tried to accept that he'd covered up everything to protect them.

The phone rang, startling her. A glance at the clock told her it was time for Lucky's nightly phone call. Their conversations sometimes went on for hours. But not tonight. Somehow she summoned up the courage to answer the phone.

"You should have seen the slopes today. They were groomed to perfection," Lucky said after their greeting. "What time will you get to Sugar tomorrow?"

Their Wednesday ski date had slipped her mind. How could she face him, or anyone, after this? "I won't be able to make it. I'm sorry. Something's come up."

After a pause, he said, "That's a shame. Is it anything I can help you with?"

"No. Some of my students need extra attention right now."

"I know someone else who feels that way."

She knew he was teasing and wished she was up to his mood, but all she could think about was keeping the secret of her family's devastated fortune from him. "Another time,

I promise."

"Em, what's wrong?"

He wasn't teasing now. She could feel his concern. "I'm fine. Just a little overwhelmed at the moment."

"I'll call tomorrow night." His voiced dropped to that intimate level she loved so well. "Sweet dreams."

She hung up the phone, staring blindly. She couldn't tell Lucky; everything in their relationship was so new, so fragile. She was afraid to test it. She couldn't tell her mother, at least not until she had tried to straighten out this mess.

It wasn't fair. A lump grew in her throat, and she forgot to breathe. Tears wet her eyes before she finally let it all go. She cried and cried, sitting in her grandfather's chair, in the house owned by two banks, in front of a folder which spelled out in black and white just how bleak her future was. She had never been so alone.

Chapter 12

Early the next morning, she had a plan. Not a good one, she reminded herself, but a first step.

"Would you mind if I take over paying the bills?" she asked her mother during breakfast.

"Of course not, dear. Did the accountant say something to upset you?"

"It was more his attitude," she hedged. Like her grandfather, she wanted to protect her mother as long as she could. "I feel like clearing out some things. Would you care if I sell the Mercedes and Grandfather's BMW? It seems redundant for the two of us to have four cars. You can keep the Lincoln and I'll use the Audi."

"Good idea. They don't get driven much," her mother said, finishing her meal.

"While we're at it, I think it's time to get rid of the medical equipment since I plan to move into that room."

Lynette stood. "Feel free to do anything you think is appropriate. Today's my day at the hospital so I have to run. I'll be having dinner with Harley so don't wait for me."

"You've seen him a lot lately," Em said.

"Do you think it's unseemly?"

The stricken look on her mother's face urged Em to her feet. "Not to me," she said, hugging her. Lynette and Harley had been inseparable during the days since the snowstorm. She never did ask how that evening had gone.

After Lynette left, Em called a number of car dealers for estimates on the two vehicles and accepted an offer from the dealer her grandfather had patronized. The money would do little toward paying off the debts, but at least the insurance and taxes would stop. They would be over that afternoon to pick up the Mercedes and the BMW.

A medical equipment supply business off the mountain agreed to come by and put in a bid for the contents of her grandfather's bedroom. She'd never committed to donating it, Em justified to herself. Lucky would just have to understand.

By that night, her panic from the day before settled into a gnawing worry. She managed to talk to Lucky and ignore the pangs of guilt over not disclosing the calamity in her life. Although she wanted to pour out her problems to him, she held back. He didn't need to know. Over the next two days, all her spare time was spent analyzing the files. There had to be a way to become solvent.

~

"This January thaw gives us a chance to go to Spruce Pine tomorrow if you want to," Lucky said during his Friday night phone call.

"I'll drive to your house since it's on the way."

"It'll be muddy so wear old boots and pants. Put away that designer stuff you always wear."

"It's all I own," Em responded.

Lucky didn't have a come-back for that. "Our backgrounds are so different. I had never even seen designer clothes other than ski outfits before I met you."

"They're only clothes, not something to be concerned about."

"That's easy for you to say. One of your cheaper dresses would be a month's pay for me." He knew his insecurity was showing, but he couldn't help himself.

"I'm not asking you to buy me any clothes. What brought this on?"

"I think about you all the time, Em," Lucky said, afraid he'd gone too far, exposed too much of what he felt too soon. He heard her swift intake of breath and, in that moment, knew what hope and fear was all about.

"I think about you, too."

She hadn't shot him down. "Now I'm a happy man! How early can you get here tomorrow?"

"Nine—and you'd better have coffee ready."

"I'll even add a pinch of cinnamon, just for you."

She hung up and headed downstairs. Laughter floated up to meet her. Delightful laughter. In the living room, Em stopped, enchanted out of her thoughts. Her mother was humming, laughing, dancing with Harley, a sprightly rendition of the Cha-Cha to music from a portable stereo.

The lightness of the moment for her mother contrasted sharply with the financial burdens haunting her. Rather than interrupt, Em held still while the music played on and the two stared into each other's eyes. She'd never seen her mother so happy, almost glowing. Harley had awakened that in her mother just as Lucky had awakened something precious within her. Em quietly left the two undisturbed.

~

Although Lucky could have acted like an over-eager puppy the next morning when he saw her drive up, he jammed his hands into his pockets to keep from touching her. He wanted to play with her, all bundled up in a dark green parka. She knew she had him, he thought, but he wouldn't roll over and beg. To play it safe, he kissed her quickly then escorted her inside for coffee. They were on their way in twenty minutes in his Explorer, with Hambone in the back seat.

"As much as I like winter, it feels good to have a warm break in the weather," Lucky said, shifting into low gear to make a sharp turn. Mundane conversation was all he could manage because he could think of nothing besides having her by his side.

"No wonder so many people I know skip to the Caribbean for a few weeks at this time of year," Em said.

"What's it like down there?" Lucky asked.

"Lush and warm. I like to snorkel and look at the tropical fish. Since I've been teaching, I can't pick up and go like I used to."

"Do you miss being able to do that?"

"Not really. I enjoy teaching, much to my own surprise, and like the structure of having a job to go to."

"You don't want to sit at home and eat chocolate and do your nails every day?"

"Is that what you think wealthy people do?"

Lucky laughed. "I have no idea. A life of leisure is out of my realm of experience. I suppose they have hobbies."

"Some have causes to fight for, such as cancer research or saving the rain forest. What would you do if you didn't have to work?"

"Travel for a while. I'd like to see Alaska."

"Good choice. And then what would you do?"

"Maybe go to college."

"Why bother? You would have all the money you'd need."

"To learn something, maybe history. I'd like to know more about the big immigrant migrations to the United States, why my people settled in these mountains."

"What would you do with the knowledge?"

"Maybe teach." He looked at her and felt as if a light went on in his head. "So you teach."

"We aren't so different after all. I happen to like math but I'm not interested in research so teaching gives me a reason to keep learning. For one thing, I have to scramble to keep ahead of some of the geniuses in the class. I have one young woman who asks question after question. It's a blessing to have someone so interested."

"Is that how you were?" Lucky asked as he turned onto the private road leading to his property.

"Probably," Em replied with a thoughtful expression on her face. "I know I drove at least one professor crazy so maybe this student is payback."

Lucky strapped on a lightweight backpack which held lunch and medical supplies and gave Em a hip pack to carry water and whatever else she needed. Hambone didn't have to carry anything. "The first part of the trip should be easy since we marked the trail. Do you want to take the lead?"

Em nodded and struck out at a fast pace. Most of the snow had melted when the warm air brought in the traditional January thaw. The ground was soft and muddy. Patches of dirty snow clung under boulders and downed trees. The pale blue sky looked cold and far away from under the bare branches of locust and maple trees. After an hour, they came to the end of the markers and Em pulled out the map. "This shows we should head toward the creek," she said.

Lucky turned her around and loosened one of the water bottles. Handing it to her, he smiled. She looked so vital and pretty here in the winter woods bare of green leaves. He wanted to kiss her, just a feel-good-quick kiss but dared not.

"I think I hear running water coming from over there," Em said, pointing to the left. She handed him the water bottle, tilting it for him to drink. His lips touched where hers had just been. He swallowed a big gulp, hoping to calm himself. After putting the bottle back in its place, they walked to the creek with Hambone leading the way.

They stood high on an embankment looking down at the creek. The map showed that they should cross to the other side, but the sides were steep and muddy, the water swollen and rushing. "What should we do?" Em asked, looking up at Lucky.

He frowned at the opposite bank. "Wait here while I search for a better place to cross. Hambone, stay." Twenty yards upstream, around the bend, was a tree, uprooted long ago. "Up here," he yelled. In seconds, Hambone was at his side. Em followed at a slower pace. Lucky looked at his watch. "We'll stop for lunch in half an hour, if that's okay with you."

"Fine, but how do we get to the other side? If you think I

can walk across that tree, you need to think again."

Lucky looked at her for a moment, then said quietly, "It's just a creek, not a raging river. I'll go first and show you how easy it is."

"It must be ten feet above the water!"

"You, who started out at the top of Sugar Mountain, are hesitating over something ten feet high?" Lucky teased.

"I twisted my knee. Remember?"

"What a beautiful knee it is. Perfectly designed to bend so you can put one foot in front of the other. Come on, I'll walk slow so you can copy my movements."

Lucky helped her up onto the base of the overturned tree before turning around and taking very short steps. "Are you behind me? Don't look past my feet. Spread your arms for balance like I'm doing and talk to me."

"This is not fun. I'm going to strangle you when we get to the other side."

"Then you'd have to cross back over by yourself," Lucky reminded her, relieved that she was keeping up with him. The water tumbled over the rocks with marked contrast to the sturdy, still wood beneath his feet.

"Can you speed this up? I want to get it over with."

Lucky grinned and quick-stepped the last few steps then offered to help Em off the log. Before he could reach her, she jumped down without his help.

"That wasn't so bad. With a little more practice, I might take up tight-rope walking as my next sport," Em said as she brushed by him.

The next marker, a triple birch tree, was easy to find. At that point, the terrain became steeper and rockier. Lucky led the way and at times cut through the briars with a machete. With every chop, his arm reverberated and a dull thud rang through the air. It might have been winter, but those brambles clung to life and sprang back at him if he didn't chop down at an angle. Stopping at a rock outcropping, he wiped the sweat from his face on the sleeve of his coat.

"I can see the creek we crossed from up here," Em said.

"And there's the road you parked the truck on, but I can't find the truck."

Lucky off-loaded his backpack, sat down, and looked where she pointed. "It's to the left. Every year I promise myself to spend more time up here and every year I get too busy." He handed Em a sandwich and removed the plastic wrap from his own.

"Peanut butter and jelly?"

"Did you expect caviar and brie?"

She screwed up her nose at his second suggestion. "Are you making fun of me?"

"You can't help having a depraved childhood caused by an excess of money."

Em threw the empty wrapper at Lucky. "You're just jealous," she teased.

The remark dampened Lucky's spark like a cold mountain fog. He studied the crumpled wrapper, and stuffed it in his pocket. "I suppose I am in a way. I wouldn't trade growing up in my family for anything, though."

"I can understand that. Sometimes I feel so alone since it's just Mother and me. It would be, I don't know, 'enlarging' to have an extended family."

"You're welcome to borrow mine any time you want. Why don't you come to Sunday dinner tomorrow at my grandma's?"

"I wouldn't want to impose."

"She's been pestering me to meet you."

"You told her about me?"

"She kept complaining that she couldn't call me, that I was on the phone all night long."

Em laughed. "What can I bring?"

Wanting to eliminate all reasons for her to refuse, he said, "Not a thing. She wouldn't hear of it. She'll probably serve fried chicken so light tastin' that you'll want to lick your fingers after eating it to prolong the flavor. And country ham from Stewart Simmons over in Tripplette."

"I've heard of him. Even Andy Griffith talked about him."

"He passed on years ago, but one of his cousins still uses his method for curing hams. There'll be collard greens flavored

with ham, cole slaw, hushpuppies and biscuits, stewed toma-
toes maybe with okra if she bought any at the store."

"Is she feeding an army?"

"Well, maybe a small one. Eight or ten of us usually show
up. And sweet tea to drink and fresh pie of whatever kind she
wanted to bake."

"Do you eat this way every Sunday?"

"I haven't missed a meal in years, wouldn't dare. It would
take more effort to explain it to her, in detail, than it's worth.
Besides, I can eat light for days afterwards which cuts down
on my own cooking."

"Hushpuppies?"

"Do you mean to tell me that you live in the South and
Martha doesn't fix hushpuppies?"

She nodded, her eyes wide.

"Grandma mixes cornmeal, a pinch of sugar, some tiny
pieces of onion, then flash fries them. Mm-mm, are they tasty.
I warn you, though, it's not for those counting calories, but you
don't have to worry about that."

"Thank you."

"You'll come?" He brushed her hair back from her face.

"I meant thank you for the compliment."

"They'll love you. I need to warn you that Grandma'll ask
all kinds of questions but you don't have to answer them. Sig-
nal me and I'll rescue you. Be at my house a little before noon."

"Doesn't she go to church? I mean, I thought all older Southern women went to church."

"After Grandpa turned up missing, she had a falling out with
the preacher and refuses to go back. She gets her church from
TV." Lucky finished his sandwich and glanced at the map while
Em ate hers. She broke off little pieces and put them in her
mouth instead of biting into the sandwich the way he did. Was
that the "proper" way to eat a sandwich? He didn't ask. He'd
look mighty silly eating dainty pieces, but on her, it looked natural.

Suddenly she shivered. "Are you cold?" he asked, berating
himself for letting them sit so long in the cool weather. As long as
they were moving, the air felt warm. Hambone let out a long,

low growl. "Easy boy," Lucky said, patting him on the head.

"No," she said, then looked around the immediate area. "I leaned into a cold spot, like you run across when you're swimming in the ocean. It was like a shadow blocked out the sun, only the sky is overcast and there is no sun." She gave a short nervous laugh. "Now I've frightened myself. Are you ready to move on?"

Lucky nodded, a little spooked himself. "Our next trip'll be quicker because we won't have to search for the markers we've already found. Seems to me, this is the same trail Grandpa brought me on once not long before he disappeared. If I'm right, the old homestead is above us, not far from a spring."

They continued in a zigzag uphill fashion because it was too steep to climb straight up. Lucky stopped frequently, claiming to have a problem with his calf but it was really to let Em rest.

"Your great-grandparents' place?"

"Farther back than that. We've been in these hills since the early 1800s. Grandpa only left here when he fell in love with Grandma and settled near her people."

The gurgle of running water increased as they walked on.

"It's around here somewhere. There—the chimney's still standing." He stepped over the low stone wall, all that was left of the foundation, and took off his backpack. He lent a hand to help Em over the wall.

"It must have been a small place. Your living room's larger than this whole cabin."

"Yeah, well, needs were different then. No exercise room, no electronic entertainment area, not even a separate kitchen." Lucky knelt down and looked up the chimney at the old blackened stones. What was it Grandpa had said? Sometimes a man had to go through fire to find the key. Lucky'd never understood what he meant.

"What are you doing? You'll get all sooty." Em bent over, glanced up the chimney. "I don't see anything but black." She wandered away.

Lucky leaned against the opening and reached up as far as his arm allowed. "Grandpa did this. Must be something up here."

His fingertips sought a niche, a loose stone, something different along the inside wall. He glanced at Em as she bent over and replaced a stone from the foundation.

Wait. His fingers moved back over the last few inches. A stone moved under his touch. He wiggled it loose and let it fall. He pressed his cheek against the chimney to lengthen his reach. Something. "There."

Em looked up. "What? Where?"

Lucky grasped a round object and brought it into the light. "A Prince Albert can."

Em walked over. "That's a chewing tobacco tin."

"Right. Grandpa's brand. It's been in there a long time." Lucky dusted it and himself off before twisting the top. "You want to see what decades old tobacco looks like?"

Em wrinkled her nose.

Lucky opened the rusty can. It was empty.

"No treasure there," Em said and patted him on the shoulder.

Lucky sighed and almost tossed the tin into the fireplace. He paused and looked closely at the scratches inside the lid. "Not so fast," he murmured. Etched inside was a rectangle with an arrow pointing to a Y. Underneath the arrow was "E62."

"What in the world?" Em looked closer. "Is it a code?"

"Maybe. Grandpa never was direct." He looked up at Em but then noticed a darkening sky. He slipped the tin into his pocket. "We'd better make a move if we want to reach the end of this map. It can't be much further."

They used stepping stones to cross the creek and stopped at the base of a particularly steep pile of stones, reminding Lucky of the gravel and sand piles the department of transportation kept around for road repair. Only this one looked like an old landslide. Small trees and rhododendron grew on it, but the pile had an unusual shape, more like the ones a crawdad leaves on a creek bank.

"Em," he said in a voice tight with excitement, "I think we've found it."

Chapter 13

Em looked around. "Found what? I don't see anything."

"I think we're looking at the bottom of a pile of mine tailings. Look at this," he said, picking up a loose handful of rock. "Have we come across anything like this before?"

"No. What kind of mine?" Em asked as she looked up the hill.

He looked up also but couldn't make out much more than the general shape because of the scrub growth. He also noticed how dark it was getting, and safety was always on his mind. "It's getting late. Do you want to climb up this now for a quick look or wait until next time?" he asked, turning to face her.

A wicked gleam came into her eyes. "Last one up cooks dinner!" Her laughter rang out as she scrambled to get ahead of him.

"Hope your housekeeper has an easy recipe in her file. You're gonna need it." Lucky headed up and easily paced himself beside her.

Her foot slipped on the loose gravel and she was down before Lucky could stabilize her. "Oh, no. It's my knee again."

"How bad is it?" he asked, slipping off his backpack.

"Give me a minute. I don't think it's serious." She straightened out her leg. "It'll be okay."

"That settles it. We'll come back another day. First we need to get you back so I can put ice on that knee. Good thing you had taped it."

She sighed and looked up the hill. "We were so close. I'm sorry I was so clumsy."

"It's my fault for not warning you about that loose rock. Can you walk?"

"Yes. It's not that bad. We'll have to go slow."

"We're still splitting the loot fifty-fifty, aren't we?" Lucky asked, intending to tease.

She hesitated before answering, "Of course. We agreed." She glanced away, then turned her back on the hill. "I'll lead us back. I should be able to follow all the markers we tied to the trees."

Lucky whistled for Hambone to join them, and they retraced their steps. Lucky asked constantly about her knee but she said it was just a mild ache. When they came to the creek, Em paused only briefly before crossing on the overturned log. They didn't talk much and made it back to the Explorer in under ninety minutes.

"I didn't get lost, even once," Em said as she took off her hip belt.

"Good job especially since everything looked different from the opposite direction. Are you a descendant of Daniel Boone by any chance?"

Em smiled. "Not hardly. How long do you think it'll take for us to hike in next time?"

"If we push, it'll take a little over two hours to the top of that mound. Weather permitting, we can come out next Saturday." After seating her in the Explorer, he removed the tape and inspected her knee. It had only mild swelling.

"I'll put it on my calendar," she said, just a little too brightly.

He activated a chemical ice pack and instructed her to keep it on her knee. Something more than her knee was bothering her, he realized. It seemed strange that she wanted to lead them back when she was injured—almost as if she was testing herself.

While driving back to Banner Elk, it hit him. He didn't want to spoil their growing rapport but the more Em studied the road signs, the stronger the feeling got. "Don't tell me that you plan to come back here by yourself."

"Okay. I won't tell you."

"I don't believe this! Besides the fact that it's dangerous to climb alone, you're after the treasure. You want to renege on our deal and keep it all yourself." Lucky's normally low-key temperament rose to a slow burn while he waited for her to deny it.

"How can you think that?" she asked after a too-long pause. "I never said anything of the sort. Why, I wouldn't have made it this far without your help."

"Not to mention the fact that you'd be trespassing without my permission. I can see it now. The Mitchell County sheriff carting you off to jail. You'd have to call your mother, of course. Or maybe you'd simply call your lawyer and keep it from her. What a juicy story for *The Watauga Democrat*. Local Heiress/ASU Professor Arrested."

"All right, all right. For a moment, only a moment, I did entertain the idea, but I discounted it right away. I couldn't do that to you."

"Why not?"

"Because we're practically lovers!" she spat out.

Lucky's anger cooled but wasn't completely gone. "Lovers?"

"Definitely more than just friends."

"Does that mean I excite you?"

"Sometimes."

"When?"

"Whenever I'm around you. Whenever I think about you."

All suspicious thoughts against her disappeared. If she enjoyed him that much, she couldn't do something sneaky. The world for him again glowed with possibilities.

~

Em wasted a large part of Sunday morning trying on different outfits to find the one appropriate for a casual afternoon dinner. She would meet not only Lucky's grandmother, but also more cousins and other assorted relatives.

"This isn't like you, dear." Her mother strolled past the bed strewn with discarded clothes. "After all," she said dryly, "your exact words were 'it's Sunday lunch, not tea with the Queen.'"

Em paused before taking off yet another dress to frown at her mother. "How was I to know my emotions of today would take over my logic of yesterday? I can't understand why I'm so worried about this."

"Could it be Lucky means more to you than you realize?"

She didn't want to think about it. She didn't dare. "We're just friends, like you and Harley," Em said, continuing her search for the right outfit. When she failed to hear a confirmation to her "just friends" statement, she poked her head out of the closet. "What about you? Taking a man to church could be seen as a serious step."

"Don't start teasing me, young lady. It's no more serious than the family dinner you're attending."

Em didn't want to hear about the symbolism of meeting his family. They were just friends, she reiterated to herself. "It's a free lunch," she quipped. Only that morning she'd asked her mother for a list of the magazines she really read and Em planned to cancel all the subscriptions her mother didn't want. When she found out that she'd been paying for the *Wall Street Journal* delivered to her accountant's office, she immediately cancelled it.

"You're not after a free lunch," her mother said.

Em pulled out a jade cashmere dress and put it on.

"That looks good on you, dear."

"I'm tired of searching," she said, evaluating the fit in a mirror. "This'll have to do." She turned to her mother. "You look good yourself. Radiant, in fact. I'm sure we have Harley to thank for that." Em studied her mother's blushing denial. Love couldn't happen that fast, especially to her mother.

After Lynette left, Em finished dressing. Her mother had changed during the past few weeks since she'd met Harley.

The biggest change was laughter—she'd always been too serious. Then there were the long telephone conversations with him. Thank goodness the house had two phone lines or she'd never get to talk to Lucky. Em wondered if she should put a time limit on her mother as she'd done when Em herself was a teenager.

~

It shouldn't have surprised Em to find her palms sweating as Lucky drove them up to his grandmother's house. She clutched a bouquet of flowers she'd brought for a hostess gift. Her first impression was of a white clapboard house built in a square with a big porch across the front. Covering almost a third of the porch was an orderly stack of firewood, positioned near the door for easy access. Smoke rose from the cinder block chimney, and Em could hear children's voices from inside.

"Relax," Lucky said when he opened the Explorer door for her and took her hand to help her out. She was thankful that she wore lined leather gloves so he couldn't know her hands were damp. "They're here to eat a meal, not you. That pleasure is reserved for me."

Em managed a tight smile for him, then softened it into a genuine one. His relatives would ask a few questions, be polite, then return to their own interests until dinner was served. Then attention would be on the food, wouldn't it? She'd be old news by the time the salad was served.

The door opened as they came across the yard, and a black-haired teenager grinned at them. "Reba," Lucky murmured in Em's ear. "Cousin, nice kid."

Reba bombed into Lucky's middle with a fierce hug. As he freed himself, she reached out a hand to Em. "Are you Emerald? Welcome!" The clear blue eyes scanned a fast and probably highly accurate assessment of Em's clothing, apparently with intense approval. "Come on in! It's cold out here."

Her smile was friendly, and Em relaxed a bit before being blasted with the sweltering heat from a wood stove. She removed her gloves and coat which disappeared into a room in the back.

Reba said in a low voice, "Lucky didn't warn you about the heat, did he? Old folks never seem to be warm enough."

"Emerald, I'd like you to meet my grandma, Cora Tucker," Lucky said, guiding Em past children putting together a jigsaw puzzle in the middle of the wood plank floor. A tiny woman with white hair bent forward in her chair with a puzzle piece in her hand.

"Land sakes, Lucky," Cora admonished, holding out her hand to be helped up, "how come you got all gussied up?"

Em glanced at Lucky and realized that he'd dressed up for her, knowing she'd be overdressed.

"Because I knew I'd be in the company of some beautiful ladies and I wanted to be noticed."

Em could have kissed him right there. He was always on her side, except those few moments he was suspicious on the trip back from the mountains.

"Balderdash. Hello, Emerald," Cora said.

Em held out the flowers. "These are for you."

"Aw, thank you, honey. Ain't they pretty? I'll go put them in water before they wilt. Introduce her to the others while I'm gone," Cora instructed Lucky before turning to shuffle to the kitchen. Lucky watched his grandmother and frowned. Em saw that the woman had a hard time walking.

Lucky introduced her around then reached down and dragged a boy to his feet. Em held out her hand, John-Michael shook it and said, "Great-grandma always said it was a shame to kill living flowers just to dress up the indoors."

Em flushed and searched for something to say. She'd committed a second faux pas.

"I think they're right pretty," Reba said, earning a grateful smile from an uncomfortable Em. Reba looked down at the boy and added, "Thoughtful gifts are always welcome."

Cora returned from the kitchen and placed the flowers in the center of the well-worn table. "This'll brighten up the room." She smiled warmly at Em.

There was a quick knock and the door pushed open. "Hope there's room for two more," Wes said as he and his wife Suzanne made their way into the room.

"Always room for you newlyweds," Cora said.

"I think we've graduated from that status," Wes said as

Lucky hugged Suzanne.

Lucky then put his arm around Emerald. "Wes is my cousin and that makes Suzanne kin. This here's Emerald."

Wes grinned. "Saw you a couple of weeks ago on the slopes. Watch out for Lucky. He likes to play doctor with all the girls. At least that's what I hear tell from my sisters' friends."

Suzanne shook her head. "These two must have been like bear cubs when they got together as kids. Growling, climbing, chasing each other. The stories Wes tells about Lucky only rival the tales Wes' sisters tell about him."

"Come on in and have a seat," Reba said. "Dad wanted to ask you about that hiking trip where you two met."

"Don't get him started," Suzanne said, handing her coat to one of the children. "That bear get's bigger every time he tells the story."

"Make yourself at home. Dinner'll be ready in a jiffy." Cora turned to Reba. "Honey, could you give me a hand?"

"I'd like to help," Em offered.

Reba looked at her doubtfully, "You're our guest."

"Perhaps I could set the table."

Reba nodded and the two headed for the kitchen. "That's a beautiful dress."

"Thank you. It's from Donna Karan."

Reba smiled. "It's nice to have a good friend who's the right size to loan you clothes."

"What?" Em asked.

"Your friend, Donna Karen. None of my friends have clothes that nice."

Em was saved from a reply as they reached the kitchen.

"The silver's in that drawer, plates are to the right of the sink. I'll put ice in the glasses," Reba told her.

The drawer held knives and forks of many different designs. None were silver. The plates were of three patterns, some chipped but serviceable. Em counted out the necessary place settings and carried them to the table. Reba was finishing up with the glasses and napkins, little paper ones, at each place.

Lucky came up behind her and put his hand on her waist,

calming her rattled mind. He whispered in her ear as she set down the first plate so that it lined up a finger's width in from the edge of the table, "I think you have a fan club."

Em looked at the two children sitting quietly where she'd left them with the puzzle on the floor. Both watched her every move. When she smiled stiffly, they both looked away.

"They aren't usually this still. You've cast a spell on them." Lucky squeezed her waist. "Just like you've done to me."

"Does that make me a witch?"

Lucky chuckled. "No, just a beautiful damsel in need of a knight." He returned to the living room.

Soon, Reba called everyone to the table. They stood in a circle and held hands while Cora said grace. Lucky squeezed her hand just before they sat down to eat.

"What's the fork above my plate doing there?" John-Michael asked.

When no one answered, Em said, "It's for dessert after the meal." Pairs of eyes stared blankly back at her.

"How come I have two other forks?"

Lucky spoke up. "The outside one is for salad and the one closest to the plate is for the main dish. It'll do us good to learn a few table manners."

"Why?"

"In case you get invited to a formal dinner sometime. Grandma, please pass the biscuits," Lucky said, and food started getting passed to Em faster than she could dish it out. She'd made yet another mistake but silently thanked Lucky for coming to her rescue. When she ate dinner, it was always arranged this way. How was she to know that everyone else didn't do this for a Sunday dinner?

"Dig right in," Cora said. "If you waited until we all finished serving ourselves, we'd be here 'til supper time. This crowd loves to eat. I always thought a woman showed her worth by the quality of her cookin' and keepin' house. Don't you agree?"

Em had just taken a bite of the flakiest biscuit she'd ever tasted. Lucky grinned when she looked at him for help. The man was going to let her fend for herself. After she swallowed, she realized everyone waited for her answer. "I can see you rank right up there with the masters."

Cora beamed.

When Lucky opened his mouth to speak, Em glared at him, daring him to say something about her cooking. He wisely said nothing.

"Grandma's pies are always the first to go at the fire station barbecues. It's a little friendly competition the ladies have," Reba said.

"Hush up," Cora said. "Let her eat."

There was no way she would ever fit in with this family. Immediately, she admonished herself for the premature thought. She and Lucky were just friends.

It wasn't until plates of hot blueberry and apple pie were being passed around that Em realized the women were clearing the dinner plates and serving dessert. It was obviously a practiced and well-coordinated operation. Apparently you kept whichever flavor you wanted and passed the others on. Suzanne scooped vanilla ice cream from the carton for those who wanted it. Em tried to help clear the dessert plates, but was shooed out of the kitchen with the excuse that she was a guest.

"Besides, you don't want to get anything on Donna Karen's dress," Reba said without a trace of guile. "How about you help the little 'uns with their puzzle."

Lucky stayed by her side for a while, but one of the cousins had a new truck and, with a helpless look to her, he followed the rest of the men out to admire it. A couple of hours after the meal Lucky, began his goodbyes. After Reba retrieved Em's coat from the bedroom, Em noticed one of her gloves was missing.

Cora saw her distress and motioned for Em to follow her into the bedroom. "It might have fallen off the bed where we stacked the coats. Let's take a look."

Em found the glove, then noticed the wallpaper. Cora followed her line of sight. "Those started showing up right after my husband disappeared."

A chill ran down Em's backbone upon closer inspection of the unusual wallpaper. Cora had plastered the wall in neat rows of check receipts from the same bank Em's grandfather had used. Her accountant's signature was on every one of them. They were bank checks, she found to her relief. No individual's name was printed on them. She walked along one wall, past the corner, past a window and saw they stopped mid-wall next to the armoire. The last check was dated last year.

"Blood money," Cora said. "I can't prove it, but I can feel it in my bones. My husband would never have left me willingly. I cashed the checks but kept these receipts. Did Lucky tell you about my Olin?"

Em nodded and walked over to her. "I'm so sorry. It must be very difficult not knowing what happened to him."

"He was a good man who loved his family very much. Lucky's a lot like him, only smarter. Olin never finished high school. 'Course, in these parts, not many people did in those days. Lucky's taken college courses and uses a computer." Pride was evident in her voice.

Em looked out the door at Lucky talking to one of his uncles. Like his grandpa, Lucky would love deeply, when and if he fell in love, she realized with a wistfulness that surprised her. His family would come first, before riches or fame. "He is a good man," she said, mostly to herself.

"Only he's too trusting sometimes. One of these days, he's gonna get burned. It might destroy him." The impact of the speculative gleam in Cora's eyes hit Em, making her blush. All she could do was nod sagely.

Chapter 14

As far as Lucky was concerned, dinner was a success. He enjoyed every minute of it. Being by Em's side brightened every day. "How about an afternoon fire and a relaxing movie while that meal settles?" Lucky asked.

"I don't think I could do anything more strenuous than that for a few hours. Dinner was delicious."

Lucky smiled at the compliment. "*Dirty Dancing* starts in about ten minutes. Have you seen it?"

She shook her head. "That came out in the late eighties, didn't it?"

"That's the one." After they'd arrived home and greeted Hambone and taken off their coats, Lucky asked, "What's wrong? You've been quiet for the last few minutes."

Em denied a problem but didn't smile.

His family was overpowering at times, but they'd been

easy on her. "Don't worry about setting the table differently than we're used to." Holding her in his arms, he wanted to right whatever was wrong. He knew it had been a gamble to introduce her to his family when they hadn't known each other long, but he was so taken by her that he wanted his family to feel the same way. And they did. "John-Michael plumb fell in love with you the moment you walked into the house. And Grandma told me you were a 'right nice lady.'"

"She said that?" Em looked up at him.

"She told me to treat you right and not to let other things get in the way of spending time with you."

"I liked her too," Em said, closing her eyes.

"Now what's wrong? You can tell me."

Em sighed and opened her eyes. "I keep thinking about how much in life she missed because your grandpa disappeared. She can't seem to let him go."

"None of us can. It might have been different if we could have had a funeral to say goodby." When he started to pull away, Em hugged him back. The warmth from her hands penetrated his dress shirt, urging his thoughts to the present. "It's good of you to feel sorry for Grandma but she wouldn't want it that way. She lives in the here and now. The past is with her, but it doesn't control her life." He took her hand and walked her to the living room.

"Good for her," Em said with more enthusiasm than she'd shown since dinner.

Lucky excused himself and made a quick change of clothes. When he returned, he said, "I left some jeans and a shirt on the bed in case you wanted to get more comfortable."

While she was in the other room, Lucky fixed coffee and lit the fire. His heart almost stopped beating when he saw her emerge from his room wearing his favorite flannel shirt. It would be forever changed after this.

"Even after that meal, these jeans are a little large for me," Em said, standing in front of him as he sat on the couch. When she tugged the waist band out to demonstrate a three-inch gap, he peered down and saw her green silk panties.

His mouth went dry, and his jeans suddenly tightened around his hips. Kissing the exposed area of her skin just below her navel, he smelled roses.

"Naughty boy," she admonished and playfully tapped him on his head before tucking in the shirt and sitting beside him.

"Are you ready to dance dirty?" he asked as the movie started.

She snuggled up against him and curled her legs up onto the couch. "Which one of us takes the lead?"

He looked down at her face so close to his. "I'd better let you make the first move," he whispered. She leaned toward him and glanced at his lips, then parted hers. He moaned just before closing the distance between their lips.

He'd wanted to do this all day, all week—ever since he met her. Just touching her lips sent tingles of temptation through his body.

His hand slowly explored the area from her waist to her ribs, then paused just under her breast. The heel of his palm pressed in to give her fair warning.

She deepened the kiss. He wanted this to be special for her, as it was for him. Sex, by itself, wouldn't feel right. He needed to be physically connected with her so she would know him, know that she belonged with him. He wanted to make her his.

With trembling fingers, he fumbled for the buttons on her flannel shirt. Damn shirt must have sealed itself up. It was never that hard to find the buttons when he wore it.

He noticed a change in the way she kissed him. First it was a break in the rhythm. Then her body shook but not with passion. She broke contact and merrily laughed, for an inordinately long time, in his opinion.

"Are you laughing at me?" he asked as he looked down to find the elusive button.

"Yes," she said and passively watched him struggle with the button. "What are you going to do about it?"

Rather than continue fiddling with her buttons, he thought of a better idea, one that would give life to a recent fantasy. "Why don't you take off your shirt for me."

"Only if you do the same," she replied.

"I like that deal." Lucky lowered the volume on the TV and let the Sixties music play in the background. He whipped off his tee shirt in record time; he didn't want to miss a moment.

Emerald stood in front of him as he leaned back into the couch. The rough fabric scratched his bare back, stimulating nerve endings.

Swaying with the beat, she unbuttoned one button at a time. A part of him wanted this time to last; another part wanted her fingers to rush to the bottom button so she would reveal herself. His own fingers curled into his palm, itching to touch her. Her gaze became a caress when her fingers released the last button.

"You're a tease," he said hoarsely.

"Only for you," she whispered then let the shirt slip down her arms to the floor. She leaned over him and he kissed the swell of her breast above the silk bra.

"That feels so good," she whispered, and chuckled deep in her throat..

"Is this what I have to look forward to with you? Laughing while trying to make love?" He kissed her again. "I could get used to this."

They made love in the afternoon while Hambone snoozed on the floor and music played in the background.

Afterwards, as they lay with his front to her back on the couch, Lucky's insides hummed with pleasure. Life was perfect and the possibilities unlimited.

All of a sudden, the emergency speaker went off, and he felt Em tense up. "Ignore it," he said and squeezed her tight.

"What about your record? You've never willingly missed a call."

"This is too special to give up. You're too special."

She turned over in his arms. This time, they made slow, sensual love and he explored every inch of her body.

"I wish you didn't have to go," he said later before they had to get dressed. "Lie in my arms forever."

"That's a little impractical. How would I brush my hair and

who would manicure my nails?"

Lucky smiled then became very still. "I love you. I want you to know that."

She started to say something, but he put a finger over her lips. A declaration of her love was all he wanted to hear, and he was afraid she wasn't ready for that.

"It feels like a bright warm sun is here, in my chest, radiating rays of love in all directions. You did this to me." He put her hand over his heart.

Em frowned. "How can you know I'm right for you?"

"This feeling is too strong, too good to be false."

She buried her face in his chest and whispered, "What is love to you?"

Lucky propped his chin on the top of her head. "It's way beyond caring, beyond wanting to be with that person. I think about you all the time. Your concerns are my concerns."

She lifted her face and looked into his eyes. "But how do you know?"

"I recognize that this is what my grandparents had. But it's different than the love I have for my family."

"I've never even imagined that kind of love."

"Until now," Lucky said, lowering his lips to hers.

Chapter 15

Emerald caught herself singing in the shower the next morning. A rare form of happiness washed over her as the shampoo lather slid down her back and into the drain. *He loves me,* her heart sang when she dipped under the spray to clear the soap from her face. *I'm the center of his universe. I'm the witty one that makes him laugh,* he'd said. She dismissed the niggling guilt of not telling him the truth about being suddenly deep in debt. Just thinking about it might jinx his love.

Drying off in front of the mirror, she studied her face, then her body, looking for an outside change to match the one inside. But the only difference she could see was in her eyes. They sparkled back at her in the mirror. She could hardly wait until Lucky finished work for the day. "He loves me," she said aloud, awed by the prospect.

They spent every evening together that week, but Emerald insisted on sleeping at home in her own bed. She didn't want to leave her mother alone in the big house.

After class each day, Em concentrated on learning about the estate. Fortunately, the stocks set aside for Martha's retirement were sound. Guess she would have to retire soon. Em's own salary for the past year was in her private checking account, which hadn't been totaled up until now. The balance wasn't as high as she'd expected. That two-month trip to Japan last summer was more expensive than she'd thought. She cut up all her credit cards, except one for emergencies. Her private account would now be the only source of money for household expenses. No more new clothes, no more personalized designer perfume. Next Christmas, they would decorate the house by themselves. Lunch would come from home to save money.

Taking control felt good, in spite of everything.

She lived for the evenings with Lucky. Conversations and dinners were light, and sometimes, so was the love making.

~

"What's important to you?" he asked one evening as they lay contentedly in each other's arms.

Em squeezed him gently around his middle. "Lots of things. My mother, of course. My emeralds. My house. Clothes that look and fit right. How about you?" She hesitated to say him because their relationship was so new.

"You are," he replied.

"Flatterer. What else?"

"Hambone, my grandma and family, my health, my sense of humor. People are important to me."

"Does that make me shallow since 'things' were at the top of my list?"

"You can't help it," he teased. "Some people learn slower than others and some are flat-out retarded. It's no big deal. One of these days, you'll get your priorities straight. Then I'll be at the top of your list."

Em pushed herself up and sat cross-legged next to him. "You're not so free of things yourself. Look at this house. It's a source of pride and comfort to you," she said, tugging at the dark hair on his chest.

"True." His glance darted to the hair she had trapped between her thumb and forefinger.

She pulled gently, released, then found the hair lower on his abdomen. "You've talked about the furniture you're going to buy and the new skis and boots you're saving for."

Clearing his throat, he shifted to try to sneak out from under her hand. She tightened her grip. He yelped moving back into place. After patting the injured area, she dipped her finger into his belly button. "You're shallow here."

He sucked in his breath.

She laughed and leaned forward, slipping her tongue into the place her finger had been. "Definitely no depth here." She kissed her way down his abdomen and then raised her head long enough to say, "Let me demonstrate a not-so-shallow part of me."

"I'll never live this down," Lucky murmured.

~

On Friday afternoon when Em arrived home, Martha presented her with an envelope.

"We don't receive many formal invitations any more," Em said, opening the announcement. She noticed Martha's clasped hands and wavering smile before reading.

"Mother's getting married!"

"She is—and she didn't want anyone to try to talk her out of it. That's why the invitations were hand-delivered today. If you hurry, you'll have time to change," Martha said.

"Hurry?" This time, Em carefully read the invitation and realized she had barely fifteen minutes to get ready. "Did you know about this?"

"No, but I had my suspicions."

A brand new outfit lay on Em's bed, complete with matching underwear and shoes. The light blue silk dress flared at the skirt. Just before putting it on, she checked for a receipt in the discarded store box, There wasn't one. Someday soon she'd have to talk to her mother about their finances, especially credit cards. But not today, she realized, frantically changing clothes. Her mother had other things on her mind.

Not much bigger than a gazebo, the tiny Crystal Wedding Chapel was as tall as it was deep with a steeple dominating the structure. Tall, narrow stained-glass windows bathed the inside with rainbow colors. Em saw Lucky immediately but couldn't get to him for the crowd. Spotting her, he smiled. All concerns about her mother momentarily fled while Em basked in the warmth of his gaze. The black tuxedo emphasized his broad shoulders and trim physique, reminding her of the power in his body and the power he evoked from hers.

Interrupting her thoughts, Martha handed her a small bouquet of flowers. "Your mother would like you to stand beside her during the ceremony. She wants your support."

"Of course," Em said as she heard the first strains of music, signaling people to find their seats.

Lucky moved to her side and whispered, "Did you know about this?"

"No. Did you?"

He shook his head then smiled ruefully. "Uncle Harley gets a kick out of surprising people. I'll bet the two of them are peeking out from behind a hidden door somewhere, watching our reactions."

"Have you seen Harley?" Em asked, trying to come to terms with the hasty marriage.

"No. My instructions are to walk you up the aisle and stand near the groom. I'm the best man. This tuxedo was delivered with the invitation at the ski slope." He dug into his pocket. "Here are the rings."

Em barely had time to glance at the two simple gold bands before the first notes of the Wedding March sounded over the speaker system.

The tiny white structure was filled to capacity which Em guessed to be a dozen people. Cora was there in a beige dress with little flowers. Suzanne and Wes grinned at her. Many more people stood outside peering in the windows. Almost all were Tuckers. There were a few people Em recognized from her mother's new work at the hospital. None of the old "friends" from her grandfather's business were invited.

As she and Lucky took measured steps up the aisle in time with the music, questions arose. Why hadn't she seen this coming as Martha had? Because she'd been too preoccupied with Lucky. Was Harley after her mother's money? The joke would be on him if that were so. How could she hide their financial problems from Harley? Where would they live? She couldn't even think about supporting another person with all the debts her grandfather had left. What will the honeymoon cost? Visions of an extended world tour popped in her head, and she almost fainted.

Lucky squeezed her hand, pulling her attention back to the present. They paused in front of the pastor before turning to face the couple coming down the aisle.

Lynette wore a simple off-white dress which went well with Harley's black tuxedo. She didn't carry flowers. As they exchanged vows and rings, Em began to cry. Would her mother be happy with a man she'd known for such a short time? Now that her mother's affection belonged to Harley, Em would have to truly stand alone.

Walking back down the aisle behind the new Mr. and Mrs. Tucker, Lucky handed Em a red bandanna. "I don't carry a handkerchief."

Em had to smile through her tears at him for the thoughtful gesture. Dabbing her cheeks, she wished her mother had discussed this with her. After all, she could keep a secret. So what if she would have asked questions and cautioned her against this rash act? Wasn't that part of being family? Lucky would understand. When her weeping started all over again, Lucky grasped her elbow and led her out of the chapel and to the passenger side of her car.

"That was my kind of wedding," Lucky said. "Simple. No fuss. Only close friends and family."

"Secretive. Rushed. Spur-of-the-moment," Em added, her tears suddenly dried.

~

Lucky parked at Chetola Resort for the reception. "They love each other—you can see it when they're together. Uncle Harley will take good care of your mother. Don't worry."

"I'm sure he will, or he'll answer to me," Em grumbled as they walked in.

Within minutes, Em cornered her mother. "I know you've been avoiding me."

"Not on purpose. It's been so hectic. Were you surprised?"

"I was hurt that you didn't confide in me."

Her mother hugged her as she'd done so many times in Em's life when she'd needed the comfort that only a mother could give. "We didn't want a fuss, as Harley called it. We wanted our wedding to be simple and quick."

Almost Lucky's exact words. Was that a universal desire men had?

"Neither of us wanted to spend any more time apart than we had to. Can you understand that?"

Only too well, she silently replied, softening her attitude and thinking of Lucky.

"The big wedding I had with your father was appropriate at the time." Lynette walked to a window, giving the two of them more privacy. "That was a merger, in a sense, and I was merely a pawn for the powerful. Don't misunderstand me, I was a willing participant."

"This time, you wanted something different," Em said to urge her on.

"Yes. Harley is warm and considerate. He brings me out of my shell. He broke my 'shell' and I'll never go back to the timid way I was." She gripped Em's hands. "Passion. He gave me the gift of passion for living."

Em's eyes widened. She wasn't sure she wanted to hear about her mother's sex life.

Lynette smiled. "Not that kind! I mean the joy of looking forward to every day. I'm more alive now than I've ever been. I refuse to waste another minute. Harley and I are embarking on a life-long adventure together. Be happy for me."

Em nodded and swallowed the lump of loss in her throat. Her mother was leaving her behind. She could be noble about this. "It's so romantic. I'm glad you didn't elope just to save a few days."

"We considered it." Her mother's laugh lightened Em's mood.

"Where are you going on your honeymoon?"

"Hawaii for two weeks. We don't want to be away from our volunteer work too long. The hospital needs us." Lynette looked away and met Harley' eyes.

Em could almost feel the air tingle between them. She would have to find some way to finance the trip for her and her new husband. Maybe she could sell some of her emerald collection.

"Besides, that's all Harley can afford," her mother whispered as she left to go to Harley.

Em gulped. At least some of the financial worry about the trip was gone. Her mother still had credit cards. Now all she had to do was accept the fact that she was now Lynette Tucker. One last toast, and the two left for the airport.

"Now what do I do?" Em asked Lucky moments later.

"Celebrate the union of two wonderful people," he said, handing her a glass of champagne.

"But it was too fast," Em protested.

"I've never seen Uncle Harley so happy. Quit gnawing on that bone. Your mother has chosen a new life and I, for one, see a rosy future for them."

"Rosy?"

"As in flower-filled, colorful . . ."

Em didn't have to drive home that night. Lynette had given Martha two weeks off since her mother wouldn't be there, and Em wanted to fend for herself. She indulged herself in a whole night with Lucky. She deserved it.

~

Saturday morning proved to be clear and cool, around forty degrees when Em and Lucky turned onto the old road leading to Lucky's land. "This is our lucky day," he said as he put his radio in a pouch on his hip and let Hambone out of the truck. "I can smell it in the air."

"That's just wishful thinking that you smell. Or maybe the hot chocolate in this thermos," she said, offering it to him, proud that she'd fixed it herself in Lucky's kitchen.

~

Traces of snow showed up as dirty white patches in the woods when they hiked back to the mine tailings they'd discovered a week ago. "Be careful," he said. "This rubble isn't as stable as it looks. Let's circle over to the side and skirt the loose part."

Two hundred feet past the base of the rubble, Lucky turned into an opening in the rhododendron and headed uphill, stopping periodically to give Em a hand up. Even through gloves, his touch sent warm sparks through her. She followed him as he angled in toward the rubble and hiked practically straight up, it seemed to her. They had climbed for half an hour when Hambone rushed up ahead. Within minutes, Em heard barking.

"He's probably spotted a rabbit," Lucky said, then called to his dog, "We're coming, Hambone. Forgive us two-legged people for being so slow."

Em looked at Lucky and grinned. As if on cue, the two of them ran the last yards out of the woods. Hambone stood at attention in front of the gaping mouth of a mine. The opening had been hidden from below by a haphazard row of bushes growing just below the crest of the rubble. Em slowed her pace then stopped altogether. The interior was black, charred in fact. A cross beam five feet inside had fallen down.

"We won't be going in there," Em said, disappointed.

"Oh yes we will—at least a few feet." Lucky switched on a flashlight he'd taken from his pack. "I wonder what kind of mine it was." Lucky bent and walked carefully into the opening. "Gold?" His voice echoed faintly.

"I doubt it," Emerald said, peering around him. The stale smell of old, wet burnt wood filled her head, chilling her to the bone. "Most of the gold was found east of here. It could be industrial feldspar or mica."

"Or garnets or sapphires." Lucky turned and patted Hambone on the head. Pebbles fell to his feet. He glanced up at the overhead beams. "Don't go in any farther, big boy. Find us something out here."

"Either way, we've wasted our time." She backed out of the mine, disappointed. She'd counted on finding some kind of treasure.

"I wouldn't say that," Lucky said, pulling her to him, wrapping her in his warmth. "I know more about my land than I ever did before. I half expected to find an old liquor still out here. Rumor had it that my grandpa operated one, but Grandma stoutly denied it."

"Maybe he operated this mine," Em offered. "Someone did."

He propped his chin on top of her head. "If he did, he didn't make much money at it. They had enough money for staples but not for luxuries. I can remember Grandpa spending hours under the hood of the pickup coaxing it to go an extra few miles. I suppose they could have scrimped and bought a newer truck, but he loved that one."

Tilting up her chin, she looked at him. "Like you feel about your truck."

Lucky laughed. "Unfortunately, no. With the mortgage I'm carrying, basics are all I can afford." He rubbed his hands up and down her arms, energetically at first, then in a more leisurely manner.

"You have a gleam in your eye that's not been put there by the thought of gold," Em teased, half wishing they were back at his house.

"Who do you suppose put it there?"

It always thrilled her that he wanted her any time, anywhere. What was more amazing, was that she wanted him. An educated, level-headed, analytical woman she was. But not when Lucky was around. It was more than lust. A longing was beneath it all.

"I'm innocent," she protested. "My actions today have not been enticing in the least. I've behaved as a partner." An involuntary glance at his lips lingered, bringing a tingle to her own.

He lowered his lips to hers. "You've been very professional." Just a light kiss. "No extra sway to your hips."

Hiking and swaying don't go together, she thought, tilting her chin for a longer kiss. Neither do kissing and prospecting.

"No deep sigh that swells your breasts and derails my thoughts," he said, framing her face with his hands.

"Do I do that?" How disconcerting.

He nibbled on one corner of her lips. "As if you didn't know."

She nibbled back, then sighed. At his knowing look, she shook her head to deny any purpose other than to fill her lungs with air.

He grinned, releasing her. "Enough of this, let's look around since we're here. Who knows what we might dig up?"

Em left his arms, feeling sexy after their flirtation, and wandered around, eventually picking up a rock. "Lucky, come and see this," she said, excitement building inside her. She showed him a gray rock with bumps. "Those are emeralds in matrix. They may not look like much to you." She wet her finger and rubbed the bumps, exposing a dull green crystal. "They're small, maybe three millimeters, but they're definitely emeralds."

"You have your wish—Emerald is surrounded by emeralds," Lucky said. "Show me what to look for."

They searched for a few minutes when Lucky reached into his pocket and pulled out the tobacco tin. He held up the lid and turned to face the mine shaft. He looked east and paced off sixty-two yards. Em and Hambone followed him into the woods. He stopped at the base of a double oak, one limb broken off above the Y. The trunk had rotted long ago, leaving a cavity. Lucky dropped to his knees and cleared debris and dirt from the space.

Lucky's fingers scraped on something metal. Em sat down and helped pull out the stones. "It's probably an old saw blade," she said, tossing rubble aside.

"Your pessimism is showing." Lucky brushed dirt away from a double handle. He paused and Hambone whimpered.

"What's wrong?" Em asked, staring in the hole and seeing nothing but old metal.

Chapter 16

"I've seen those handles before." Virtually attacking the stones holding down the box, Lucky worked until the hole was a couple of feet deep. Tugging at the two-foot long narrow box, he managed to loosen it from its grave. "This thing must be filled with rocks!" he said when his first attempt to lift it failed.

Shifting one knee to use as leverage, he hefted out the box which landed with a thud on the loose stones. With apparent reverence, he rubbed along the handles and the top of the metal container. "This was my grandfather's."

"How do you know that?" Em asked, perplexed as to why her grandfather's map led them there.

"This tool box was a memento from World War II. He was a mechanic with the motor pool somewhere in Europe."

"It could have belonged to anyone. Those can be bought at army surplus stores." She didn't want to get her hopes up.

Lucky didn't know that this could be the key to stabilizing the Graham finances.

"If I'm right, his serial number is engraved on one side of the lid. He glued the German and English coins he'd found in his pocket after his tour to the other side of the top."

Em reached and flipped one side open. Inhaling swiftly, she raised her gloved hands to cover her mouth. "Oh my God."

Lucky flipped open the other side. "Emeralds!" he exclaimed. "Lots and lots of emeralds." Tearing his gaze from the stones, he winked at Em. "Now I'll be as rich as you, partner."

"Does that mean so much to you?" Wealth had never seemed important to him.

"No, but it would make me more your equal." He looked down at the box.

"Who's keeping score? I'm not. My worth can't be compared to yours. Look at all the lives you've saved. Don't ever put yourself down in front of me again." Men and their egos.

"Whatever you say, ma'am."

Returning her attention to the box between them, Em giggled nervously and picked up one of the green gems. She no longer heard Hambone's panting as he lay on the gravel beside her or the creak of the leafless trees bending in the wind. The cold air ceased to sting her nose as she inhaled. Lucky's comments faded away.

Emeralds! The stuff of her dreams. She closed her eyes and rubbed a cool smooth crystal against her cheek. If she could have inhaled it, she would have. She rubbed it across her lips as if it were a lover. Still in the throes of her dream-like state, she opened her eyes to see Lucky staring intently at her. Startled, she jerked the gem from her face, nearly dropping it.

He must think I'm crazy, she thought. As a cover, she babbled, "This is museum quality. It's a perfect hexagonal prism, well-terminated and with good, dark green color." She handed it to Lucky, reluctant to let it leave her fingers.

"It must be an inch in diameter," he said, holding it up to the light.

"See how the color is uniform and almost transparent. It doesn't have any foreign inclusions or fractures." She reached for another one, looked at it, then inspected another. Most were like the stone they'd picked up outside the mine—small green bits embedded in rough matrix, but others were gem-quality crystals. Each was different yet beautiful. She wanted—no needed—to handle each one, to hold in the palm of her hand. As her heart pounded in her chest, she imagined they were all hers. Yes, hers! Not to sell or because they were valuable, but because they were beautiful. The map belonged to her grandfather. She glanced at Lucky and shame filled her heart.

Here was a trusting, loving man whose main purpose in life was to help others. How could she have considered for even a moment that they weren't in this together?

After dropping the stone in his pocket, Lucky took off his gloves and touched the coins glued to the top of the metal box. Half expecting to see the ghost of his grandfather, he looked up. All he saw was Hambone sniffing rocks on the other side of the mine entrance. "I remember giving Grandpa a new Sears Craftsman tool box for Christmas one year. He made a production of cleaning all his tools before transferring them from this box to the one I gave him. I wondered what happened to the old one."

"This solves that mystery," Em murmured as she picked up another stone from the top shelf.

Lucky lifted out the shelf and revealed even more emeralds. The answer to his money problems gleamed up at him. His grandma could have her operation and pay her back taxes; he could furnish his house; and Hambone could eat the best dog food available. "Partner, this is worth a small fortune."

"We'll have to have these appraised."

He narrowed his eyes wondering why the sudden caution on her part. "What was Grandpa doing with all these emeralds?"

"And why did my grandfather have a map leading here?" The corner of an age-yellowed envelope shone bright against the olive-gray side of the tool box. Tugging gently, Em pulled the envelope from under the stones. There was no writing on the outside. Her fingers shook as she tore off her gloves and slit the edge of the envelope with her thumb nail. The page crinkled as she unfolded it.

The signed contract was on a half sheet of paper. It was nothing but a statement that the two men agreed to work as partners and split the profits—in Everett Graham's scrawling script—and signed with both names. Em doubted it was legal, but what mattered was that it tied her grandfather to Lucky's unmistakably.

Lucky took the page and read it. He stared at Em as he handed the paper back.

While Emerald looked at the page in shock, Lucky's reaction to the contract was eclipsed by a much more important thought. Lucky ran to Hambone's side and dropped to his knees. "What is it, boy?" A chill ran down Lucky's back when the hair rose on his dog's spine. They shivered in tandem. This spot felt colder than the surrounding winter air.

They both dug in the dirt—claws and fingers moving frantically with determination. Lucky found a large flat rock and used it like a shovel to scoop out the dirt. It was slow going. He didn't know if this was the right place, but he needed to take action, needed to *do* rather than think. Anything but think.

"What are you doing? Can I help?" Em asked but didn't move from her spot.

"I'd rather do this myself," Lucky said without pausing in his work. Your family's done enough, he thought uncharitably. The only sounds in the woods were those of the make-shift shovel moving dirt and of the rock scraping against smaller rocks. He pounded the sharp edge of the rock against a small root. Hambone panted as he dug. Sweat broke out on Lucky's face. He had to be here . . . Grandpa had to be buried here.

One more shovelful, and he knew he'd have to take a break. Gasping for breath as he rested, he looked back into the hole and saw something dark. He reached in with dirt-encased fingers and touched something that was not rock or root.

Leather. "Oh, Grandpa," he whispered, shoving the dirt aside. A worn brown boot was soon exposed. Further excavation revealed a bone in the boot. Hambone let loose a long, haunting howl.

Em moved to his side but he reached for Hambone instead.

Lucky wrapped his arms around the dog and cried. Tears streamed down his face as his heart squeezed into a tight ball in his chest. He cried for all the memories he didn't get to share because his grandpa had died too early. He cried for the hard times his family had endured. Most of all, he cried for himself.

After a while, his tears dried up. He was drained. "I've got to call the sheriff. I've found a body." His voice sounded as heavy-hearted to his ears as he felt.

Em scrambled to her feet. "Wait. Do we have to? I mean, this happened so long ago. Couldn't we work this out ourselves?"

Lucky narrowed his eyes to stare into hers. She flinched.

"What would people think of my family if news of this got out?" she asked.

"I'm sitting at the grave site that will probably prove to be my grandpa and you're worried about your reputation." Lucky hissed, standing to tower over her.

"Think of my mother and your uncle. He's part of my family now," she pleaded.

"Think of my grandma. Her faith in her husband's loyalty is proven at long last." He clenched his fists at his sides. The injustice of it all. He'd fallen in love with a woman whose family had tried to destroy his. And now, she didn't want anyone to know about it.

"I wouldn't dream of keeping this from your family. But the newspapers will seek out and print every grisly detail."

"That can't be helped. The sheriff will probably confiscate the emeralds and tool box as evidence," he added, watching the blood drain from her face.

"The contract too?"

"Of course." Lucky turned his back on her and lifted the

radio from the holster hanging from his belt. He punched in 911. Static greeted him. He walked out into the open and repeated his call.

"Sheriff Adams here."

"I found a dead body on my property. It was buried here years ago," Lucky said after a few words of introduction. He gave the location of his truck and added, "You'll have to hike in a few miles, but the trail is clearly marked with orange surveyor's tape." The sheriff promised to leave within a half hour. It would take that long to assemble the necessary people.

When he finished the call and turned back to Em, he sucked in his breath. His intention was to go to her, to tell her that they could work out the details, that he would stand by her family through the upcoming news blitz, that the sins of an earlier generation did not get passed on. But the look on her face hardened his heart. She was almost as bad as her grandfather, he thought, as she crouched over the emeralds in the tool chest, tears streaming from her eyes. All she was concerned with was the loss of the emeralds. The death of his grandpa didn't mean anything to her.

Chapter 17

"Oh, Grandfather," Em whispered, clutching the box. "How could you do this? How could you live a lie for so many years?" Gradually, her tears stopped and she sat in the snow-covered gravel while the sheriff and State Bureau of Investigation agent worked around her. Was this somehow her fault? Had her birth influenced her grandfather to refuse to reduce his lavish lifestyle and give his partner the money that was his?

Naming her had been his little secret, she realized with disgust. At that moment, the sheriff clenched the handles to the tool box nestled on the ground between her legs. "What?" she asked, frowning.

"It's evidence, Ms. Graham. I need the paper, too."

"Yes, yes. I understand." Em let go of the box and paper as if they burned her. Even her name was tainted. She couldn't bear to look at Lucky. How he must hate her. "Do you have any questions for me?" Em asked Sheriff Adams, not caring that her voice was weak.

"I'll need for you to come in and make a statement. Tomorrow'll be soon enough. It'll be late by the time we finish here. You can leave whenever you're ready."

With dread in her heart and lead in her feet, she forced herself to walk over to Lucky. The officials were still digging up the grave, but Lucky hadn't moved as he stared down at the bones. The flash from the photographer's camera barely made him blink. Em inched closer to him, careful to keep her eyes on him and not to let them stray to the ground. She didn't want the sight of the grave seared into her memory. Coping with the idea of murder was difficult enough without having a visual reality check.

"What's this?" One of the diggers stabbed into the dirt beside the bones. He broke up the dirt in a long line parallel to the bones then used his hands to brush away the clumps.

"Well, I'll be hanged." The sheriff ordered photos before reaching down and picking up the slender item. "Looks like someone wanted to hide the evidence. Mighty convenient for me. All I have to do is find out who this belongs to. It's a beauty— or was." He wiped the dirt from a rifle and inspected the stock. "Highly figured cherry stock. Only one man in the mountains does work like this. I'm sure he'll recognize it. I haven't seen a bolt action 30-06 like this in a long time. Winchester model 70. Has a Leupold variable scope." He handed the rifle to an officer to be wrapped as evidence.

Em gulped. She couldn't be sure, but it looked like some of those her grandfather owned.

"Can I take the wedding ring to my grandma?" Lucky asked the sheriff.

"I'm sorry, son. The forensic specialists will need that as well as the boots and other clothing fragments to identify the body. That'll probably be enough. No need for a DNA test."

"I'll bring it to your office tomorrow."

Sheriff Adams shook his head then stopped. After consulting with the SBI agent, he returned to Lucky. "Agent Liles has agreed to go along with you to your grandmother's and have her identify the ring. That's the best we can do. We have to keep it until the investigation is over."

"How long will you hold the evidence?"

"It could take two to three months, maybe less. An old case like this can't be top priority. However, since you're sure of the identity, it's more a matter of dental and x-ray records. The autopsy should confirm that the death was caused by a rifle shot to the back of the head," the SBI agent said.

Em's stomach tightened at his last words. "Murder," she whispered.

Lucky looked her full in the face for the first time since he'd discovered the body. His shoulders drooped, his eyes held compassion, and his hand started to reach out for her.

When Em extended her hand, he froze. To her horror, her fingers held a forgotten emerald that glistened in the fading light. "I didn't keep this on purpose."

His eyes clouded with confusion then cleared with resolve. "Didn't you?" A grieving and caring Lucky transformed before her eyes into a hardened stranger.

"Can I get a copy of the contract tomorrow when I go in to give my statement?" Lucky asked the sheriff.

"I don't have a problem with that."

"Do you?" he asked Em.

She slowly shook her head, feeling trapped in his gaze. Later, she couldn't remember the hike back to the truck. She only remembered that no one spoke.

Once they were on the road, she cleared her throat. "I want you to have all the emeralds, my share too."

Lucky snorted. "Trying to buy me off?"

Would this nightmare ever end? "No. It's the least I can do to try to make up for this." Inadequate maybe, but it was everything she had to offer. Maybe she should tell him about the estate and get all the bad news over with at one time. One glance at his stony face changed her mind. A better opportunity would present itself.

"It's mighty generous of you. But why are you doing this?"

"I—Grandfather did a terrible thing. Those emeralds were

mined by your grandpa, and you should have them. Please don't make this any harder than it is." She turned her face from him, not wanting to expose her anguish any more than she had to.

"Okay. I accept. But this doesn't affect the rest of the estate. They'd been partners for years. My guess is, about that time, Grandpa had dug emeralds worth millions. That box was merely the latest. An audit of your grandfather's accounts could prove that. At the least, Graham stole a million from us. You owe us, big time. Grandma will have her due."

Em nodded. A headache pounded in her head, adding to her misery. It wasn't until Lucky pulled into Cora's drive that Emerald snapped out of a fog of dark thoughts.

"I'll wait here." She sunk further into the hard seat of the Explorer, prepared to sit in the cold for as long as need be.

"That's what you think." Lucky slammed his door, tromped around and jerked open her door. "Grandma has had faith for a long time that her husband did not abandon her. You have to witness this moment. Your family owes her that."

"What's wrong?" Cora yelled from the porch as the sheriff's car came to a stop next to the Explorer.

Em's step faltered. Lucky pressed his hand into the small of her back to propel her forward. If only she could disappear for ten minutes, this would all be over, she thought as they walked onto the porch. It wasn't fair. None of this was her fault. But guilt piled up inside her anyway.

"Grandma, I want you to come inside and sit down."

Cora covered her heart with both hands. "Is it your uncle?"

Lucky opened the door and urged his grandma into the living room. "No, but it is serious. We have something we want you to identify. This here's agent Brian Liles with the State Bureau of Investigation."

Cora's eyes widened. She looked from face to face and sat. Em saw the blood drain from her proud but weathered face, saw her chin tremble, and saw Cora press her lips together, obviously marshaling her inner forces for what was to come.

Em straightened her spine and did the same.

"Ma'am," the agent said, unzipping the plastic bag. "Can you tell me anything about this ring?"

Em sucked in her breath, almost feeling the stab of pain that registered on Cora's face. Em clenched her fingers into a fist when Cora took the simple gold wedding band in her hand. A flush crept up Cora neck. Tears welling in her eyes, she adjusted her glasses to try to read the inscription on the inside of the band.

Not a sound was made in the room. Even the winter wind was still. Em's heart beat loud and fast in her ears as she watched Cora blink several times, refusing to give in to tears.

"Where did you find this?" Cora whispered.

Lucky knelt before his grandma. "Down in Spruce Pine on that land Grandpa left me."

The agent cleared his throat before asking. "Do you know who the ring belongs to?"

Cora nodded. "I put it on my husband's finger. He promised me he'd never take it off."

Em's legs buckled, and she collapsed into a chair. Lucky looked at her but didn't move. His first concern was his grandma, Em thought. But she could use a comforting hug right now, like the one they'd shared in front of the fire at his home.

Cora glanced at Em before addressing Lucky. "How did you find this?"

As Lucky explained about finding the map, following it to the emeralds, and finally digging where Hambone had pawed, Em shriveled inside. Her grandfather was a part of her; his genes guided her and would influence her children, if she had any. How could she ever hold her head up again?

"Emerald," Cora said, patting the seat beside her on the sofa, "come over here."

Em grabbed Cora's hand as if it were a life preserver. "I'm so sorry this happened. I had no idea."

"Of course not, child. It was your grandfather's doing, not yours. I don't blame you in any way, and you shouldn't even consider taking on that guilt. You had nothing to do with it."

"You are so kind." Em looked down at Lucky still kneeling in front of Cora. She couldn't read his eyes. Neither hate nor love radiated from him to her. It was as if he had closed in upon himself.

"How long will they keep my husband's things?" Cora asked the agent.

"Two to three months, at the most."

"Including the emeralds?"

When the agent gave an affirmative reply, Cora and Lucky had a silent exchange. "Bring me the Bible," Cora instructed her grandson. Lucky returned after a trip to Cora's bedroom with the large, well-worn volume. Em sat mesmerized as Cora's rough hands caressed the embossed cover. The gilt on the page edges had worn off in places indicating generations of Tuckers had read and reread the contents.

Lucky handed Cora a pen. Although her hand shook, the pen strokes were even as she wrote in the blank area beside Olin Tucker's name. His death date was forever embedded in the family archives as well as in the hearts of those present. Then her worn, loving hand wrote "murdered."

Em wanted to die.

Cora cleared her throat. "I knew he wasn't carried away by no aliens like some at the church said. I never asked him directly, but I thought he worked undercover for the government. He complained about people growing marijuana on these mountains, so I figured his job was to find the stuff and report it."

Em held still, afraid that anything she did would only make matters worse.

"Once those checks started coming, I knew better. I cashed them but kept the receipts as a reminder. It was blood money, all right. A rich man's way of tryin' to buy his way into heaven."

After the book was returned to its proper place, Cora took one of Em's hands. "I know this is hard for you, but how long will it take for you to get your assets in order so we can get our half of the money from all those years my Olin worked that mine?"

Em blinked in confusion.

"We have some rather pressing expenses coming up and this is an answer to our prayers."

Jerking her hand free, Em stood and struggled to think clearly. She meant the money. Half of all her inheritance. Half of all her debt. Em nervously laughed aloud. "I was worried about how you would react about news of your husband, and all you can think about is money." She hadn't meant to go so far, to be so disrespectful.

The look of concern left Cora's face. "I was thinking about the cost of the funeral, which will probably be in the neighborhood of seven thousand dollars. My husband will have a proper funeral."

"Of course he will," Em said, chagrined. "I can advance you that."

"I don't borrow or take charity. The Tuckers take care of their own." Cora's lips pressed into a thin line.

Em looked helplessly at Lucky who frowned before saying, "I think we better talk to a lawyer."

A cold fear seeped into her heart. Losing Lucky now that she'd started caring for him was more than she could bear. Thinking and feeling would have to come later. She had to get out of there. Now.

Em looked at the agent who said, "A lawyer is a good idea. Even a judge in civil court may not be able decide this one. It'll probably go to a jury."

A jury would mean even more publicity. The entire state would know about her grandfather's crime. Oh, Lucky, what should we do? He looked as undecided as she felt. "I guess that's the next step," she said. Her treasure had turned to more than just ashes, it had toppled her entire world.

~

Lucky drove her home. When they reached the house, he cut the Explorer engine and leaned back in silence. Em had run out of apologies. She could not change the past and undo the hardships his family had endured because of her grandfather.

"What about us?" Lucky asked.

Of all the questions she'd anticipated, this was not one of them. "I wish I knew."

"What would we be doing if none of today happened?"

Em stared out the windshield, afraid to look at him, afraid to see what she had lost. "I would be kissing you right now, wishing we were at your home, in your bed." She heard his swift intake of breath.

"This isn't the way I expected the day to end."

The bleakness she felt shone in his eyes, but only for a moment.

Like a door slamming in her face, resolve hardened his face. "I can tell you don't want to give us what's rightfully ours. Your estate means more to you than justice."

Her heart almost shut down at his coldness. Edging away from him, she met his eyes. "I guess the lawyers will be in charge now." At his nod, she got out of the truck and walked, refusing to turn and watch him drive away, possibly for the last time.

Chapter 18

Monday afternoon, as Em came out of the Graham Math Building, two TV crews and several newspaper reporters surrounded her.

"Is it true millionaire Everett Graham murdered prospector Olin Tucker?"

"No comment." Em walked fast, seeking the sanctuary of her car.

"How did you feel when you saw the bones?"

She hoped her sharp intake of air was not detected. It was an ugly question. "No comment."

"What do you think of Cora Tucker's statement, 'We're glad to be able to put my husband to rest in a proper grave.'?"

"She has grieved and suffered long enough. Why are you so interested in this ancient story?" By this time, she'd reached her car.

"Graham heavily influenced North Carolina governors and senators in the 90s. Anything involving him is headline news."

Her hand shook as she inserted the key in the ignition and drove away. Quake-size shivers racked her body so hard she had to pull over after driving only a mile.

The next morning at the University math department meeting, only a few people greeted her. Conversation stopped when she entered the room, only to begin again after she sat by herself in the back. One friend finally sat next to her and asked if she was okay. Em nodded and blinked back tears that seemed so close to the surface these days. She didn't know which reaction was harder to take—being ignored or facing someone who was overly nice.

Unless she found something hidden in her grandfather's accounts soon, she'd have to tell the truth. Either way, it was time for her to view teaching as a career, not just a hobby. Thank God she enjoyed her job and changing students' attitudes toward math. Maybe it wasn't too late to sign up for summer classes. Vacations would be out for the rest of her life.

After the meeting, she went home and wrote want ads to sell her sports equipment. Except the skis. She couldn't part with those—not yet. Her mountain bike wasn't that old and should be worth at least a thousand, half what she paid for it. Best offer was all she could advertise for the mountain climbing gear. Tennis, golf—had she really put that much money into sports? Never again, she vowed.

Next came her closets. The consignment shops in Charlotte would be the closest ones for her designer clothes. Around Boone, she knew she'd only get a few dollars for each piece. Tourists and college students couldn't care less about them. Fingering the green cashmere dress longer than necessary, she forced herself to put it in the "to go" pile. After that, the pile grew quickly. If she didn't need it for teaching, she didn't need it at all.

~

Saturday morning when Lucky knocked on Em's door, a subdued and wary woman greeted him. "We have an agreement," he said, striving to remain unaffected by the dark shadows beneath her green eyes. Green for greed, a fitting color for her family motto, he reminded himself to shore up his resolve. "I always live up to a contract to restructure a closet, regardless of who is involved. Besides, we need the money to pay for the funeral."

"I offered—"

"We refused. After all, soon we'll be getting our rightful inheritance."

Without a word, Em did an about face and led Lucky to her former bedroom. He noticed the remodelers had finished in her grandfather's room the week before, and she'd lost no time in moving in. "I believe this room was next," she said stiffly.

"Still spending our money freely, I see." The room had been prepped for painting.

"This was contracted months ago, you know that." The words grated on his ears as if forced through clenched teeth. "I also honor my agreements."

"That's good to know." He chuckled then said, "Grandma's already spending her share of the inheritance. A million bucks, wouldn't you say? Did I tell you? She's decided to divide Grandpa's money into equal parts, one for her, one for Uncle Harley, and one for each of my uncles. That way, the immediate heirs can figure out how to pass it on if they want to."

"That means you won't get any."

"Grandma figures I deserve the emeralds. As I recollect, most of those in the chest weren't gem quality. But some were. Money from the sale of those will go a long way in paying off my mortgage. Maybe you can help me. What type of furniture should I buy?"

Em narrowed her eyes. "I wouldn't plan too far ahead if I were you."

After she left the room, Lucky's forced arrogance left him. His defense had been met by hers, so they remained in a standoff. All morning long as he measured, nailed, and installed shelves in the closet, he railed at the injustice. Objectively, he knew Em hadn't caused any of it, but he also knew he couldn't act logically yet. His family had been attacked and someone had to pay.

His whole life had been lived under a shadow he hadn't deserved. He remembered the elementary school kids' taunts that his family was so bad the grandfather ran off. The weeks of shivering under winter blankets because cash was so tight they couldn't use electric heat and the wood stove couldn't heat the whole house. The shoes he'd worn even after they cut out the toes to make room for growing feet.

Em had probably worn a new outfit every week. Hunger and cold were as foreign to her as charge cards and easy credit had been to him. It was his life that had been cheated.

Em picked the wrong time to walk in.

"I could have gone to medical school." He stood clenching his fists in frustration and faced her.

Clearly caught off guard, her mouth dropped open. Recovering, she said, "You could have applied for a scholarship."

"Don't be so naive. College-bound people have to be raised with the expectation of going. I had to concentrate on working just to help with the bills. Do you have any idea what it's like to have to work sixty hours a week?"

"I do have a job, if you recall."

"All you've ever known is school. You were sent to boarding school and never left the protected ivory tower. I'm surprised you allowed yourself to get your feet dirty by walking with me," he taunted just as the kids had done to him years ago.

"What's wrong with living in the world of new ideas, ancient philosophy, and intelligent people?"

"Not a thing if avoidance is your game. You look down from up high on the less fortunate." Lucky looked down his nose at her to emphasize the point. "Messy emotions screw up the logic and order of your life. You act like compassion is foreign for you."

"That's not true!"

"You wouldn't even leave that box of emeralds to help me uncover my grandpa!" His voice practically exploded from him. "That isolated little vision of yours never strayed from the money. No ma'am. The thought that I might need you at that moment never even entered your mind." His words echoed in the empty room as he struggled to gain control of himself.

Em's eyes widened. "I came over to you but you grabbed Hambone instead of me!"

"I don't remember that. All you cared about was the treasure. I saw it in your eyes—all green and shiny like those stones."

"You bastard! I was thinking about what my grandfather did."

Lucky's eyes burned into hers as the first two words she'd yelled echoed in his ears. Classmates had used those same words in describing his father. They were wrong, of course. But what did kids know?

Their stares grew into a standoff, an awkward silence. Emerald blinked first and looked away. "I'm angry, too. At first, I denied the evidence." Em's hand shook as she brushed her hair back from her face. "The grandfather I admired and respected had murdered and cheated for money. I loved a man who never existed. My love meant nothing. Nothing! Don't you see? He cheated me, too."

Lucky tried, really tried to muster up some sympathy for her situation, but his own emotional needs overshadowed all else. Her strident voice sounded sincere. The fire in her eyes looked real. His lawyer had said she might make a bid for concessions against half the inheritance. He'd warned him of tears, sexual favors, even trickery to keep her money. Not that the lawyer knew Em. He simply said that everyone changes when it comes to large sums of money.

Em took his hand between hers and drew it to her heart. "Please believe me. I was too stunned by the news to pay attention to what you were doing. I would have helped."

"I'm trying to believe you," Lucky said, but the lawyer's advice stuck in his mind. He stepped back, forcing her to drop his hand. "Speaking of your grandfather, Grandma wants you to see that Olin Tucker's name is added to any plaques, awards and scholarships given since our money was used for those." Lucky looked away, his stomach clenched at the dismay in her eyes. Damn. He should have let the lawyers handle that one.

"But that will take a lot of research. I wouldn't know where to begin."

"Begin with those stock market people from the party. Call his accountant. Go through his files. It's little enough to ask considering that a man's life was cut short way too soon."

Em took a deep breath. "I'll see what I can do. Here's a check for the two closets. Our contract called for three so I'll pay for this last one when the work is complete."

Lucky took the check and frowned. "This is your personal check. You told me the household bills were paid by the accountant."

"I fired him." Em lowered her eyes. "Besides, my lawyer advised against my using the other accounts until things are settled between us."

Her words struck at his heart and he almost regretted paying any attention to his lawyer. Then he looked around and saw the splendor she'd been raised in. Silks, antiques, even leather bound books. She may not have caused the problem, but she certainly benefitted from it.

"Lucky, this isn't really between 'us.' It's between our families. I'm not the bad guy here. And neither are you." The shadows under her eyes and her subdued manner hurt him more than he expected. He reached out to her, but she misunderstood his gesture.

"No. You keep the check. It's better this way."

She was right, he thought after she'd left the room. Keep it impersonal until the estate was settled.

~

Later as Em was again going over the accounts, her eyes filled with tears. Lucky had been so close to her. He'd needed a shave. His eyes looked tired. If only she had a magic wand and could take them back to the beginning of February. She longed to have his arms around her, to feel his heart beat in his chest. She missed his kisses and the sparks that flew between them. She missed feeling so alive when he was near.

Em sighed and walked around the library to try to get her mind off Lucky. She'd have to trade the Audi. The dealer had found a used Subaru four-wheel drive car that would be cheap enough to eliminate payments. It couldn't be helped.

The phone rang and Em was surprised to hear her mother's voice on the line.

"I thought you two didn't want to be disturbed on your honeymoon," Em said with forced enthusiasm.

"It's different if I do the calling. I had an unsettling dream last night that you were in trouble. Is everything okay?"

Em swallowed hard. "All is quiet at the moment. Is Hawaii as breathtaking as its reputation?"

"It's more than can be put into words. Harley and I plan to take a helicopter ride over Mount Kilauhea . . ."

Lynette talked for a long time about their trip while Em tried to block out recent events. She would not spoil their honeymoon with her own bad news.

". . . and Harley said to spare no cost. He's such a gentleman. I've never felt so cherished, so special, so happy before." Her joy bubbled along the telephone line. "Since you've assured me that all is fine, I have to run along."

After Em hung up the phone, she gave thanks for conscientious men, their protective nature, their sometimes frustrating "macho" needs, and for their stubborn insistence on paying their own way. She'd never before understood that those qualities could be viewed as blessings.

Unless taken to extreme, like her grandfather had done. How could she ever come to terms with the part of him he'd kept hidden from her?

~

Wednesday morning dawned with grey clouds hanging low over the slopes, matching Lucky's mood. The evening before, he'd spent another restless night in front of the fire with Hambone. The dog had gone to the door at the slightest noise outside. He told Hambone that she wasn't coming.

He couldn't figure out why she was so mad at him. His family had been wronged, not hers. She was used to having money, but she really didn't crave it or actively seek it out, as he'd accused her of in anger. So why did she want to work through lawyers? His family was reasonable. Maybe the estate was so extensive and involved that she couldn't divide it up by herself. Why didn't she explain that to him? Round and round his thoughts went.

"It's just us two old bachelors," he'd said to settle Hambone back down until the next time. Even the *Ski Patrol* magazine couldn't hold Lucky's interest. After flipping through the TV channels twice, he turned off the set. Although he was mad at her, nothing distracted him from missing her.

It was hopeless, but all day on the slopes he watched for her. She had a season pass and had claimed many times this was a good way to work off any frustrations. She had to be as stressed as he was. Any woman dressed in green drew his attention. She could have bought another outfit, he thought, so he scrutinized all the skiers. His eyes and head, as well as his heart, ached from the strain.

It was so bad, he lost his temper once when he brought down the sled in response to a patroller's call. Dean had stopped the young man's nose bleed. As they put him in the sled, the man kept asking Lucky if his nose was broken. Three times, Lucky answered that he didn't know. He'd have to see a doctor. When the man asked again, Lucky snapped. "I'm not Superman—I don't have X-ray vision." Dean looked sharply at Lucky. Courtesy and patience with skiers were strong rules at Sugar.

"Are you the guy who's dating Doctor Graham?" the man on the sled asked. "I have a Tuesday/Thursday class with her."

Lucky groaned and took the sled straight down the hill as fast as he could. He couldn't go on like this. Lawyer or no lawyer, he had to see Em.

On his next trip up the lift, he saw her at the bottom of the run. He yelled her name, and she looked up at him. When he waved, she shook her head and continued skiing. If he could have, he would have jumped from his chair, but the twenty-foot drop deterred him. He got off at mid-station and skied straight to the bottom. Since it was close to closing time, he guessed Em had her last run for the day. He stashed his skis at the lift shack and jogged to the parking lot. He had to find her. Earlier at lunch, he'd spent the entire time checking the parking lots for her Audi and hadn't seen it.

As he jogged, he looked at people and cars. There! Five hundred feet ahead of him Em opened a car door and quickly got inside. The engine roared to life. He slowed down and stopped the chase when her tires threw up stones in her haste to leave.

This was ridiculous. She couldn't avoid him forever.

Why was she driving a Subaru? What had happened to her Audi? She'd once told him that it would take a catastrophe for her to part with that car. Come to think of it, what had happened to the BMW and the Mercedes? The garages at her house had been empty last Saturday, but he hadn't thought anything about it at the time.

Something was going on, and he wanted an explanation. He deserved one.

Chapter 19

Leaving work the next day before the 4:30 slope sweep was something Lucky had never done before. His surprised boss didn't ask why, just told him to go. A report in the morning newspaper left Lucky spitting nails. The reporter insinuated that Em had known about the murder. She'd fired her accountant for getting too close to the truth. Recently, she'd sold her cars to consolidate her assets before the courts could get involved.

He couldn't believe he'd been taken in by her, when he knew better—knew better—than to trust a rich, spoiled socialite who was just looking for fun. What did he have to offer such a woman? His good looks and pure heart? What a moron. And to think he'd taken her to meet his family. Brought her to his grandma's house like she was his fiancee or something. She must have been laughing at him all along. How could he have missed it?

It was those damned green eyes.

He'd been wrong about her all along. She was a money-hungry bit—He stopped himself, not wanting to insult a female dog. Here he was, walking in the footsteps of his father. He had fallen for Mom on these same grounds. It hadn't worked out well for them either.

He found the Graham Math Building, soon to be Tucker-Graham if Em had been following up on her promise, after questioning only two students for directions. Parking was impossible so he simply blocked in Em's Subaru. Up the stairs, turn left, then left again, second door on left he mentally recited.

"Just a minute," she called through the door in response to his knock. He heard two voices approaching the door. When it swung open, Em stopped mid-sentence.

She looked so good he simply stopped breathing and stared. Her hair formed a halo around her head, backlit by the window. Jeans hugged the body he knew so well.

Absently, she said to the student, "I'm afraid I need to cut our meeting short. I'm sorry. I think you're making good progress on your topic, but see if you can find a few more sources. OK, Jen? And if you need to see me again on Thursday, come on by." Her gaze never left Lucky's. The student sidled by Lucky who practically blocked the door. Lucky didn't move. He couldn't. What was he supposed to say now that he was here?

"Come in. Come in." Em grabbed his arm and pulled him into her office. She quickly glanced up and down the hallway before closing them inside the room.

Doubts assailed him. This was her space, her world. Crisp diplomas were framed on the wall. A large bookshelf was filled with books and periodicals bearing obscure titles. Stacks of important-looking papers were arranged near the computer monitor on a polished walnut desk, behind which stood a comfortable swivel chair done in butter-soft leather. "Dr. Graham," said a brass plate on her door. Who was he, to be in this Dr. Graham's world? Lucky Tucker, high school graduate, standing here in his WalMart jeans.

She and her lawyers would eat him alive.

No, they wouldn't. The Tuckers had been down and out for a long time, but their fortune was about to change. Lucky Tucker had nothing to be ashamed of. He was as good as any college professor, especially this one. She and her rotten family had made the Tuckers suffer long enough. He rounded on her.

"Why did you run from me yesterday at the slopes?" This was not going as he'd intended but it was too late now.

She exhaled a deep puff of air. "You don't waste any time, do you?"

"Not today." Might as well get it all out in the open. "While you're at it, explain this," he demanded, slapping down the newspaper articles on the desk in front of her.

"It's hard to explain, especially with you standing there, glaring down at me."

Taking a controlling breath, he leaned against a bookcase. "Better?"

She wouldn't look at him. "I didn't want to talk to you."

"Obviously. Why go skiing at Sugar?"

"I have a season pass. It's an exciting sport, and it's a good way to distract me from things."

At least he'd gotten that right about her. "You can afford a lift ticket for Beech or Appalachian. Why my slope?"

She stood and turned to look out the window. She murmured something.

He strode around the desk, "What was that?" It took all his willpower not to touch her. She was so near he could smell her rose shampoo.

"I had to see you," she whispered. "I watched you all day, but I stayed out of sight."

His lungs and anger deflated in an instant. Why did you run from me, his brain screamed, but the question never left his mouth. His body had a better idea. He turned her and crushed his lips to hers. She had to feel the same way he did. Heart to heart, they could speak. Why did family history, education, and wealth intrude into their lives? Her arms clasped him as tightly as his wrapped her. He kissed her as though his life depended on it.

Not yet ready to talk about the real reason he came, he

settled on humor. "That kiss was better than a double-black diamond mogul run."

She raised an eyebrow.

"Better than fresh-churned butter on cornbread."

Em added in a weak voice. "Better than Godiva chocolates."

He had to think about that one, not being all that fond of chocolates.

She sighed. "Better than a ripe avaca —"

"Whoa. I'm not sure I like being compared to things."

"What makes you think I like it?" she countered.

He stepped back and stared at her for a moment. "Good point."

When Em glanced at her watch, Lucky took the hint. "What happened to your Audi? You didn't have an accident, did you?"

"No accident." She shook her head.

She's stalling, he thought. She doesn't want to tell me the truth. "Did you sell it? The newspaper said you were selling off assets and depositing the money somewhere that would be hard to trace." Deny it, he silently pleaded.

"I did sell it, but not for the reason you think. I don't know if you'll believe this but—"

He couldn't listen to her excuses. "Save it. I couldn't bear to hear any lies." He opened the door. "The SBI released the emeralds and Grandpa's effects. All the publicity speeded up the process. Grandma's operation is scheduled for next week and Grandpa's funeral is tomorrow afternoon, in case you're interested."

She nodded. "The newspapers are wrong." She cleared her throat. "I hope all goes well with the operation and . . ."

Lucky glanced at his watch, cutting her off. "I have an appointment with a jeweler in a few minutes. I assume that's the best way to sell the emeralds."

"It's a good place to start."

He nodded and left.

With her body still humming from their kiss, Em stared at the door he'd closed behind him. What had they just done?

He'd come to her mad and left the same way, but in between? She shivered, loath to make a move. As soon as he had walked in, she'd wanted him.

How could he, a family-loving, warm-hearted man, want the likes of her? Murder was in her blood. Even now, she didn't have the courage to tell him that everything was worse than he could imagine. For a little longer, let him believe she was greedy. It was a small price to pay.

Inhaling to sigh, she jerked out of her despair. At the same time the student entered, she sat in her chair, hoping she looked normal. "Have a seat, Kevin," she said, slipping her feet under the desk and her mindset into that of a teacher.

~

She drove home feeling dejected, rejected and disgusted with herself. When she saw Harley's car in the garage, dread was added to the list of dark feelings building inside her.

The first thing she saw when she walked into the living room were newspapers strewn on the floor around the couple. Her mother immediately rose and grasped Em in her arms.

"What are you doing home?" Em hugged her mother and didn't want to let go.

"Now that I'm part of the family," Harley said, opening his arms to Em, "don't I get a hug, too?"

"Of course." Em hugged him briefly, still getting used to her mother's new husband. She moved several steps away.

Lynette's welcoming smile faded into a look of concern. "Why didn't you tell me about this when I called?"

"I didn't want to spoil your honeymoon."

"Should I leave you two alone?" Harley offered.

Em shook her head and led them to the sofa. "I need to tell you the whole story. For us," she said, looking at her mother, "it is disastrous." As she told them of the recent events, practically using the same words that Lucky had used in telling his grandma, her mother looked not at Em but at Harley. It hurt, her mother's not needing her. Hearing the catch in Em's voice, her mother grasped one of Em's hands and one of Harley's. Then Em gave the details of their non-existent estate.

"So Ma was right all these years," Harley said when Em fell silent. "I'll bet she called every newspaper she knew of. You can't imagine the gossip Pa's disappearance caused. She'll want to be sure every single person who bad-mouthed her hears about this. She's a proud woman who deserved better." He patted Lynette's hand.

His wife nodded. "Why don't you call her?" She kissed him sweetly on the mouth just before he left the room.

It unnerved Em to watch her mother kiss someone, especially one of the people her family had wronged. Lynette had a secret smile on her face.

"I hate to be the one to interrupt your reverie," she said to her mother, "but we have a serious problem. I don't think you understand the implications of this."

"I understand that Harley can now bury his father and put the ancient speculations to rest."

"That also means that my grandfather—your father-in-law—was a murderer!"

Lynette sighed heavily. "I suspected that he had committed some crime, but not one as serious as this," she added when Em's eyes widened. "You see, dear, we talked a lot during his last months, but he held something back. He would be on the verge of confessing, then he'd clamp his mouth closed, almost mid-sentence. I didn't press him, but maybe I should have."

"It wouldn't have changed anything."

"Maybe, maybe not. He mentioned something about sacrificing his favorite rifle. I didn't understand at the time. He died with the weight of the crime on his soul."

"Or he died laughing through his teeth at the world. He'd lived a good life and gotten away with murder," Em said dryly, not really believing her own accusation. "Now we have to pay the consequences."

"Will we have to sell the house?" Lynette's voice didn't shake as it might have a month ago.

"Probably."

Lynette patted Em's hand. "I wish you had called us. You shouldn't have had to deal with this all alone."

"I thought you and Harley deserved a little island of peace."

"That was sweet of you, dear, but it's you I'm worried about." Lynette leaned back. "We had already decided to live in Harley's home because it's closer to his family. Martha's talked about retiring since your Grandfather died, but she didn't want to leave me alone. I don't mind giving up this big old house. I want something small enough for Harley and me to take care of."

"But Mother, what do you know about cleaning house and ironing shirts and cooking?"

She laughed. Em's heart warmed a bit at the light sound. "Almost as much as you do. But I can learn. Remember, I have a loving man beside me. It makes all the difference in the world. How did Lucky react when you told him that there was no estate?"

Em was suddenly too edgy to sit. She paced in front of her mother. "I haven't told him."

"Oh, dear."

Tears sprang to Em's eyes. "I couldn't do it. I tried, but I couldn't face his disappointment. Instead, I studied all the accounts, trying to find some hidden assets. But there were none." She blinked rapidly to clear her eyes.

Harley walked into the room. "I ought to head over to Ma's soon. I'll be glad to explain it all to her."

"We'll go to her, Harley. She's my mother-in-law now. I don't think Em needs to go along, do you?" At his agreement, Lynette stood beside her daughter. "You don't have to go to the funeral, either, if you don't want to."

After they left, Em retreated to her new bedroom. She'd failed to react well to the whole situation. To make matters worse, it was the first time in her life she'd been tested by adversity. Did she have a "greed" gene that skipped generations like the gene for twins? No, not her.

She'd betrayed her mother's trust by not taking over the family finances as soon as Grandfather had died. She'd betrayed Lucky's trust by hiding her money problems and then compounding it by keeping silent. Like her grandfather, she'd betrayed the two people she loved the most.

Her descent into self-pity skidded to a stop, as she realized the truth.

Love. She loved Lucky.

It might be impossible to resolve their differences, but she loved him nevertheless. She smiled slowly. Why had that been so hard to recognize? Why had she fought it? Giggles rose in her throat. Fly like a bird, she told herself. Thinking about him tingled her senses.

She loved that strong, brave, infuriating ski patroller. He was brave enough to corner her in her territory, in her office. Heroic enough to go over a cliff to rescue a stranger. He had to help people. It was a basic part of him.

And talented. He'd built his own house, her dream house.

She paused, not liking the direction her thoughts took. If she didn't live there, another woman would. Someone else would sit before the fire. And share his bed. With trembling fingers, she brushed back the hair from her face. The truth about her mistake would hurt him. His own dreams of inheriting the Graham riches would die. After she sold the house, only a few hundred thousand would be left for his family. She could sell her own emeralds, the ones her grandfather gave her for her birthdays and Christmas. They must have come from the mine. Dealers wouldn't have to know they were blood-tainted.

But she must face him. Now. First, she must explain herself, apologize for her mistakes, and then she could hope to be forgiven. He couldn't stop loving her now that she realized that she loved him. Could he?

She grabbed her coat and headed out the door, praying that he was home and not at his grandma's. Harley only spoke about Cora and hadn't mentioned Lucky.

Chapter 20

"Who's at the door, Grandma?" Lucky called from her bedroom. Wiping the gum off the wallpaper scraper, he stepped back to critique his work. Each of those check receipts had to be taken off separately since that was the way they had gone on.

"Come see for yourself."

Frowning, Lucky walked to the living room. Immediately, he grinned at his uncle. "I thought y'all planned to stay in Hawaii longer'n this." Crossing the room in two strides, he gave Lynette a bear hug before slapping Harley on the back. "Missed us too much, I'll bet."

Harley's half-hearted smile cooled Lucky's enthusiasm.

"You heard about Grandpa?"

"We did. Ma, Lucky, we have something to tell you. Let's all sit down." Harley took Lynette's hand and sat on the sofa. His serious tone tightened Lucky's throat. "Did something happen to Em? Is she hurt?" Their last words had been an argument. If he had caused her to do something rash . . .

"No, she hasn't had an accident. Sit down and hear me out."

"Hush, child, let your uncle speak," Cora added.

She was safe. Lucky couldn't sit but nodded for Harley to begin. From the look and tone of Harley, Lucky knew he wasn't going to like the news.

"To begin with, there is no big estate."

Lynette interrupted her husband. "My father-in-law's sins included the major one of murder as well as a minor one of lying to his family. By the time he died, he was deep in debt and never told me. We're selling the house which should bring a few hundred thousand."

Cora and Lucky tried to speak at the same time but were stopped by Harley. "I know. You have lots of questions so we'll take them one at a time."

Underlying all of Lucky's thoughts was one question: why didn't Em simply tell him? With half an ear, he listened to the discussion as he paced about the room. The money didn't matter to him. Of course, it was a disappointment to his family, but his life would go on the same as before.

What he couldn't figure out was—why had she kept silent? He'd been wrong to think she wanted to keep the money herself. The newspapers hadn't been any better than he had in investigating. But he didn't think he needed to check out her motives. She should have trusted him. Was the truth so hard for her to face?

He hadn't asked a single question. Didn't need to. The signs had been there that she wasn't spending money, but he hadn't seen them.

By the time he realized the others were leaving, he'd worked himself into a fit of frustration. Mad at himself for not realizing she was in trouble. Mad at her for not facing up to him. He walked out the door behind his uncle and drove home. The wallpaper could wait. If he didn't work this off with hard labor soon, he'd do something he'd regret.

~

"Thought she could find a secret account!" he mumbled as he took out the sledgehammer and set the wedge in a piece of wood. The hard blows of splitting firewood should take some of the fire out of him.

"Wanted to protect her mother!" Bam! The piece split cleanly in half. "Regret her actions!" he yelled, taking a full swing of the hammer. Why did he waste his time on her? This was his reward for his devotion. With every muscle in his body, he slammed down on another piece of wood. And again, and again.

Only the sound of a car in his driveway gave him pause. Looking up, he saw the back end of a Subaru driving away and used every curse word he could remember, even inventing a few of his own. She'd run away from him again.

~

Friday morning went better than Em expected. Her confidence had been shaken the day before, when she was too late to confess her mistake to Lucky. Thank goodness the power she so much admired in him hadn't been directed at her. That firewood looked like toothpicks when he'd finished with a piece. Not that she could blame him. She only hoped she could still reach him.

Lynette showed the realtor around the house while Em taught advanced statistics at the university. When Em came home and faced her slimmed down wardrobe, she had no trouble picking out a black pantsuit but the closet itself was hard to face. The gleaming new shelves reminded her of him. She could even pick out the one screw she had put in.

At the funeral that afternoon, Em strove hard for composure. Deciding a path and following it through were two very different things. These people were related to Harley, and he was now family.

She couldn't let her mother down. Everyone was warm to the new bride but merely civil to Em. She felt as if she had caused the whole episode instead of merely complicating matters at the end. Suzanne and Wes nodded to her as she made her way to her mother's side. Little John-Michael and his sister stared at her. The hardest part was facing Lucky.

For a moment, just a half-second, she imagined she saw a longing for her in his eyes. Then he blinked and it was gone. She sat and her mother patted her hand. A Tucker leaned forward and said quietly, "We know this is as big a shock to you as it is to us, dear."

Tears came to Em's eyes and the service began. Em stared at the ornate casket as the preacher's voice droned on. A large photo of Olin and Cora stood at the front. His eyes bored into her. She was truly alone. Her mother had found love and Em had lost it.

Now was not the time to talk to Lucky, but she wanted the lost feeling in her heart to ease.

She had to get away. Feeling trapped, her skin crawled on the inside. Would the preacher never finish the eulogy? Panic rose in her throat. Her eyes burned and began to tear. Gripping her hands together, she desperately tried not to turn and run.

Her mother and Harley deserved more from her. Despite her efforts, her body trembled. A soothing hand reached over and touched her clasped ones. Her mother's strength poured into her and ended her panic. She could endure this. Lucky would not see her fall apart.

"Amen." She quickly dabbed the perspiration from her face and rose. "See you later, Mother."

"We're having a painting party at my—our house tomorrow. Another pair of hands would help," Harley said as she turned to flee.

"I've never done anything like that before." Any excuse would help her now.

"Don't worry about that. We'll give you the beginner's job of rolling the big walls. By the end of the day, you'll graduate to painting trim. Guaranteed."

She involuntarily glanced at Lucky. Her heart squeezed into a tight ball. Could she find a way to talk with him alone at Harley' house?

"We'll understand if you have other plans," Lynette said. "You can come and see us after it's all done. We'll have you over for dinner, if you dare trust your life to my cooking."

That did it. Em lifted her chin. There was no way all the work would be done by Tuckers. There would be Graham marks in her mother's new home.

Chapter 21

𝒜 lost-my-heart-in-a-bottle-of-beer country song blared on the radio but it didn't lighten Lucky's mood. It wasn't the work. He loved to paint and wanted to help Harley fix up his home. All the kitchen, dining room and living room furniture had been moved to the garage and to the sheds scattered throughout the property. Cabinets, doors and trim were covered and drop cloths protected the floors. Harley had removed the electrical face plates while Lucky spackled the holes in the walls.

When the final sanding and wall wiping was done, Lucky glanced at the clock again. Nine a.m. If she hadn't shown up by now, she probably wasn't going to come. It was just as well. He was too mad to be able to speak with her amicably anyway.

Coveralls on, he added a baseball cap and safety glasses. Texturing a ceiling was messy work, but he was good at it. He made sure even the corners and edges were nubby. With a paint-laden, long-handle roller in hand, he raised his arms to the ceiling and made his first swipe.

The door slammed. He jumped. Textured paint rained down on him like March hail stones. A big glob eased its way down his neck and under his collar. "I thought I told everyone to use the other door," he fumed through gritted teeth. Lowering the paint roller, he turned to face whichever relative had been stupid enough to come in a masking-taped door.

"I knocked. The music was blasting. I didn't think anyone heard me so I came on in."

Em looked beautiful in a matching sweatshirt and sweat pants, even her jacket was color-coordinated. Designer work clothes.

"Wasn't the door a little hard to open?" His voice was loud in order to be heard over the music.

"Yes, it was. I thought it was stuck."

Her tongue snuck out to moisten her lips. He knew the move was probably a nervous gesture, but he took it as something else. It taunted him. It played with his libido, his ego and his body. That little tongue had taken him places he'd never gone before. And he couldn't afford to go to again. Not with this lady. She was out of his league. She was too much work. Scandal was in her genes.

"Let me take your coat." Harley rushed in the room and pulled her past the danger-of-paint zone. "Glad you could join us."

"Sorry I'm late. The car wouldn't start. I had to find a neighbor with jumper cables—"

"You didn't call a garage?" Lucky asked, interrupting her excuse.

"I thought it would be faster and less expensive to ask the neighbor."

Harley shot a warning look at Lucky. "Good thinking. Come into the dining area and we'll get you started."

Lucky stared at Em as Harley led her to the other room, then returned to his work. Attacked the job was what he actually did. Brutally. When the painting was finished, he had almost as much on himself as on the ceiling.

She had lied to him. She'd had plenty of opportunity to explain the inheritance to him, but did she? No, she was a coward. He was better off without her.

When he moved to the other two rooms, everyone pointedly moved away and worked on the walls in the living room. Including Em. He didn't blame them for avoiding the black cloud of a mood he was in.

By the time he finished all the ceilings, cleaned up the rollers, and stripped off his coveralls, he'd calmed down. Sometime that afternoon he would find an opportunity to ask Em some logical, unemotional questions. After lunch, he managed to paint the trim near where she rolled the walls. The others were in other rooms, and he had her to himself.

"Why didn't you tell me about being broke?"

When the roller clattered to the floor at his feet, he realized that he should have worked up to that question. He should have at least spoken to her earlier instead of avoiding her.

He picked the roller up off the tarp and handed it back to her. She hesitated, obviously afraid to touch him. Reaching high on the handle, she grasped it clear of his fingers.

She returned to rolling without answering his question.

"I asked—"

"I know what you asked. I'm formulating an answer."

"Formulating? Just answer the question. Don't concoct an elaborate excuse. Try the truth for a change."

"All right!"

Her temper matched his, he realized. He kept an eye on the dripping roller she held between them.

"I kept hoping it wasn't true. I looked for a secret account. I checked all of the stocks he'd purchased over the years for a money winner. They were all worthless. I looked in his files for accidental over-payments. I wouldn't—couldn't—admit to myself that it was true."

"You didn't trust me." His voice was flat, belying his emotion.

"I didn't say that. Don't you understand? I didn't tell anyone."

"Emerald Graham can stand alone. Is that it? You don't want or need anyone else."

"You know better than that."

"Do I? People who care about each other share both the good and the bad. What did you think I'd do?"

She trembled but didn't say anything.

"What is the worst thing I could have done to you?" Still no response. "Run away? Call you names? Leak information to the newspapers? Answer me. I deserve an explanation!" He seethed in anger at her stubbornness. He reached in frustration to shake the truth from her.

She shrank back from him.

He dropped his hands and said in a hoarse whisper, "I'd never hurt you."

"I know that."

"Have I ever given you reason not to trust me? My whole life is involved with helping people. Apparently, that's not good enough for you."

"At first, I couldn't tell you because it meant facing the truth." She glanced away, then resolutely met his eyes. "My life was a fraud. My grandfather wasn't what he appeared to be. My family destroyed your family once, and now there's not much estate for your family to inherit. Of course, that wouldn't make up for losing your grandpa. If I work for twenty years, I could never replace what was stolen from you, not on my salary."

"You knew the truth would have to come out."

"I tried to tell you that day in my office. But you wouldn't let me. You walked out. After that failed, I lost my courage. I couldn't bear seeing the disappointment in your eyes. I made a terrible mistake not to trust you. I know that now. I'm trying to face both your anger and your disappointment. Is it too late for us? Can you forgive me?"

Lucky swallowed hard. What had she done that was so bad? She'd tried to rescue the family finances. She'd shielded her mother and him as long as she could. "I don't know."

Others came into the room, effectively ending their conversation. She left before he had a chance to talk to her again. It was just as well. He had some thinking to do.

~

Her mother moved the rest of her personal belongings and what furniture she wanted on Monday. Both Em and Lynette cried when Martha officially retired. She moved to her sister's place that same day. Em was thankful that the housekeeper's retirement had been in an unbreakable trust that even her grandfather couldn't touch.

A buyer had been found. In a few weeks she would vacate the house her grandfather had built with blood money. It hardly mattered any more. The place was empty and lonely anyway with her mother and Martha gone, and some of the furniture, carpets and paintings auctioned. By now it was just creepy. She hadn't found a place to live yet. It would need to be something very reasonable. She was looking at apartments in town.

After all the publicity, Everett's portrait had sold for a hefty sum to a collector of morbid memorabilia. Em knew it was disrespectful to sell the patriarch's portrait to a collector, but she figured it was the least—and last—thing he could do for them. The remaining gun collection went to a private collector; neither Em nor Lynette was willing to deal with the attention those would bring at auction.It was interesting how Everett's society friends had all evaporated overnight. She and Lynette were guilty of no crime except a sudden lack of money. Even the Tuckers had been nicer to her than Everett's money crowd.

Enough of sadness and loss, Em decided. Enough of feeling sorry for herself. She would go for a day of skiing. She packed a lunch, used her season pass, and limited her expenses to gas. She'd prove to herself that she could live within a budget.

If Lucky didn't want her, maybe she would get a dog, a small one who didn't eat much. The humane society always had photos in the newspaper of adoptable dogs. Then she wouldn't be so alone.

She wasn't going to try to see Lucky. No, the next move was his. Even though he deserved someone better, someone who had a simpler life, she wouldn't give up yet. Meanwhile, she had to adjust to cooking her own food, to making her own bed, to doing laundry. Life without her housekeeper just added one more level to the punishment she deserved. Martha wrote down everything and walked her through the domestic chores. Em's brain felt like mush absorbing all the details. Who would have thought keeping house was so complicated?

At the top of the slope, she inhaled the chilly air to bolster her spirits. The wet snow from the night before had frozen on the tree branches, weighing them down like a thick coating on fried chicken.

Great. Now she even thought like him. Moisture in the clear deep blue sky crystallized into Tinkerbell's magic dust sparkling in the sun. She could use a little magic. Exercise would energize her. It always had in the past, she reasoned. She started down the hill. The first turn was jerky, the second was easier.

What if he thought he needed someone born and raised in the area? Someone without murder and scandal in her family history. Someone who would be a natural in the kitchen, would enjoy scrubbing floors. Jealous moisture clouded her eyes. Drat. She couldn't see the slope. Blinking didn't help.

Her ski tips crossed and stopped her feet from moving. The top of her body continued downhill. Suddenly, she was face down in the snow. One of her skis automatically released and hit her in the back. Suppressing a moan, she was afraid to move. Afraid to find out that she was hurt and worried about continuing to slide down the hill.

"Are you hurt?"

Without looking up, she knew that voice as well as she knew her own. She shook her head, hoping he wouldn't recognize her all bundled up, behind the new goggles. Her hair was tucked up under her hat. This was not the way she wanted to see him again.

"Em, let me help."

"How did you know it was me?" She cautiously moved her legs so she could sit up in the snow. "Other women wear green ski pants."

"I saw you get on the lift." He stepped out of his skis and knelt in the snow beside her. He took off her goggles and stared at her until she met his gaze. "I'd know you anywhere. You're in my mind all the time."

When he brushed snow from her face, she allowed herself to hope. "I am? But I let you down."

"Your grandfather did. Once you close on the house, all the taxes, funeral expenses and Grandma's medical expenses will be covered. You and the rest of the family can split what's left. Most of all, Grandpa's finally laid to rest. All of that wouldn't have happened without you."

"What if I'm like my grandfather? I like having money." She played her own devil's advocate. She wanted him to know her as she really was. Truth and honesty meant much more to her now than before she'd met Lucky.

"Who wouldn't? Look at what you chose to do for a living. Teaching. That's not a profession for the greedy. You could have used your math skills in stocks or gambling. Instead, you decided to help others to learn."

"I didn't think about it that way."

"You never held being poor against me. Why should I hold it against you?"

"I'm not the woman you thought you met. My whole life was a lie."

"The woman I taught to ski is with me now. The one who shared my bed and my roof hasn't changed. Her bank account has, but she hasn't."

A shiver of self-forgiveness went through her as she drank from the honest devotion in his eyes. She hadn't lost him! She loved this wonderful man, but what was more remarkable, he loved her back. Not for her money—she had none. Not for her social standing—if that went any lower, it would have to go underground. But for her own self. In spite of all that had happened, all the reasons he should despise her, he still loved her. She thought her heart would burst.

"I love you, Em. Move yourself and your furniture into my empty house. Make us a home. Marry me."

After everything they'd been through, he still wanted her in his life, in his arms.

Lucky reached into an inside pocket and pulled out a small box. "When I got home after that day at the mine, this was in my pocket. I had this made for you."

Tears welled up in her eyes and she had a hard time seeing the emerald ring with detailed silver surrounding the stone. "You were mad and disappointed in me. How could you still want us together?"

"Deep down, I guess I knew we would figure out how to be together." He slipped the ring on her finger. " Besides, we could always work the mine."

"We'll always find a way to work things out. I'm so lucky to have found you."

"I'm Lucky, remember? You're my Emerald in the snow."

The End

Maggie Bishop settled in the mountains of North Carolina in 1993 with her husband and cat. Every time they travel, they seek out other mountains but none are as exciting as these ancient Appalachians.

She's an Air Force brat who put herself through East Carolina University, a former manufacturing executive, founder of High Country Writers and a hiker, swimmer, golfer and skier.

Maggie is also the author of *Appalachian Paradise*. The cover silhouette of Appalachian Paradise is of Maggie and her husband, Bob Gilman.

Appalachian Paradise

Athletic career woman meets good-ole-boy for a five-day backpacking trek in the rugged North Carolina mountains. Appalachian born Wes triggers Suzanne's resentment and her desire amongst boars, bears and Girl Scouts. Suzanne's pack and old hurts lighten as Wes' easy charm helps her truly see the hope and allure of spring flowers, love and forgiveness.

This Appalachian hiking novel is a good read for any vacation – beach, mountains or back yard.

VISIT MAGGIE BISHOP'S WEBSITE AT:
http://maggiebishop1.tripod.com

High Country Publishers, Ltd

invites you to our website to learn more about Maggie Bishop and her work. Read reviews and readers' comments. Link to Maggie Bishop's site and find out about her other works. Learn what's new at High Country Publishers. Link to other authors' sites, preview upcoming titles, and find out how you can order books at a discount for your group or organization.

www.highcountrypublishers.com

High Country Publishers, Ltd

Boone, NC
2004

Appalachian titles
from
High Country Publishers, Ltd

Where the Water-Dogs Laughed
by Charles F. Price

Fourth book in the award-winning Hiwassee saga
ISBN: 1932158502, $24.95

Appalachian Paradise
by Maggie Bishop

An unlikely romance on a five-day hike through the heart of the Appalachians
ISBN: 0971304564, $9.95

Dear Mouse . . .
by schuyler kaufman

Murder and love on an Appalachian movie set
ISBN: 0971304521, $14.95

Monteith's Mountains
by Skip Brooks

A serial killer chase set in the Great Smokies of 1900
ISBN: 0971304548, $21.95

Once Upon A Different Time
by Marian Coe

Romance on an 1884 trek through the Appalachians
ISBN 1932158537, $12.95

Plumb Full of History
by Donna Akers Warmuth

A fictional tour of Abingdon, Virginia, for the whole family
ISBN: 1932158782, $9.95

Strike a Golden Chord
by Lila Hopkins

Romantic suspense with a Christian orientation; illustrations by the author
ISBN: 1932158510, $23.95

Weave Me a Song
by Lila Hopkins

A heartwarming story of unconditional love; illustrations by the author
ISBN: 0971304572, $19.95

High Country Publishers invite you to order books from our High Country Publishers' People & Places series for gifts or for your own enjoyment. You may photocopy this page or simply send a letter or e-mail with the following information to our office.

Shipping address:
Name:
Address
City, State, Zip

Appalachian Paradise
_____ $12.00   Total: $ _____
Emeralds in the Snow
_____ $9.95   Total: $ _____
[Quantity]   [Other Titles]
_____ $ Total: $ _____

_____ $ Total: $ _____

Tax (.075% only in NC) $ _____
Shipping $3.00   3.00

Total $_____
You may enclose a personal check for the total or send your credit card information below:

(   ) VISA (   ) Mastercard

Card # _____ _____ _____ _____ Expires:_____

Signature:

High Country Publishers, Ltd
197 New Market Center #135
Boone, NC 28607
(828) 297-7127; fax: (828) 262-1973
www.highcountrypublishers.com
sales@highcountrypublishers.com